USA TOD.
Dale Mayer

Brandon's BLISS

HEROES FOR HIRE

BRANDON'S BLISS: HEROES FOR HIRE, BOOK 13
Beverly Dale Mayer
Valley Publishing Ltd.

ISBN-13: 978-1-773360-65-2
Print Edition

Books in This Series:

About This Book

Brandon, the newest member of Levi's team at Legendary Securities, heads to Africa. Bullard purchased a new holding there, but, shortly after arriving, went missing.

Kasha has worked for Bullard for five years. She's familiar with most of those who work for Legendary as well. Brandon proves his worth almost immediately, planning her boss's rescue and staying right by her side in the days that follow while they determine what imbroglio Bullard's stepped into. Accident or a deal gone horribly wrong, it seems Bullard was running guns and now his newest holding is under attack.

Their emotions, heightened by danger, run hot as Brandon positions himself instinctively at Kasha's side—which is exactly where he hopes to be permanently if they can just find a way out of this rapidly escalating mess.

Sign up to be notified of all Dale's releases here!
https://geni.us/DaleNews

Prologue

BRANDON HORTON WASN'T sure what to make of Legendary Security. He'd been here two whole days already, and so many people had been coming and going, it was hard to keep track of who was who. And then there were the puppies. Six of them—although several were going to individual apartments on the property when they were old enough. But all the homes were connected to the men who worked around here.

Brandon only really felt comfortable in a chair propped against the back wall of the huge dining room, out of the way—yet close by when meals were served. The trouble was, nobody let him stay here alone. His buddies from his former SEALs unit, Rory—sporting a new cowboy hat—and Michael, had stuck close so Brandon wouldn't feel isolated.

Also Ice had come over several times to get him to fill out paperwork. He'd done that and had passed it back and then continued to stay quietly in the background. He was getting paid, but he sure as hell didn't know why or what for. He'd expected to be shipped out on a job immediately, but so far that hadn't happened.

This was early into Day 3 for him, trying to figure out how things worked at the compound. Breakfast had been devoured and cleaned up over an hour ago. He doubted that this bunch took weekends off, so just because it was a

Saturday in early December per the calendar didn't mean he had the day off.

The phone rang. He wasn't even sure who was supposed to answer it. He knew it wasn't him. He barely knew what was going on from day to day.

When Ice walked into the kitchen adjoining the dining area, her tone clipped and urgent, the atmosphere shifted. Something was up. She turned on the big screen in the kitchen and hit an alarm on the side of the door. People poured into the room. He pulled farther back from everyone, watching curiously.

An image filled the screen. Ice keyed in something on the laptop nearby and a news ticker appeared at the bottom. The scrolling text confirmed the facial ID of the woman on the screen as Kasha Lowry, gave the GPS coordinates for her exact location in Africa—dubbed Bullard's Home Base— even compared the date and time here in Texas, within our Central Time Zone, currently 10:27 a.m., to the time some seven hours ahead in the West Africa Time Zone, so 5:27 p.m. over there.

Ice was known for her IT magic, so she had her own particular set of toys.

Brandon could see some of the room behind the woman. It looked like the command center of a big military operation. He'd never seen anything like it in a personal residence.

"Kasha, you're up. Go ahead."

"Ice, Bullard has gone missing," said the tall, lean young woman with long black hair, worry creasing her face and fatigue pulling on her features. "Six days ago, five of us traveled to his newest property on the Benin border in West Africa. He said he wanted to stay for another day alone. Get a feel for it. So he sent us away. We expected him back the next day, but, when the pilot landed to pick him up, there was no sign of him. He hasn't answered his comm. Our men are out on multiple missions, so we're shorthanded here."

"We'll send four men. Two from here and Merk and Stone who are already nearby in Europe. They'll arrive within a few hours of each other."

Brandon watched the relief light up Kasha's eyes. With her long dark hair and slightly honey-toned skin, she was a knockout. But the way she wore her tight black jeans, tight black T-shirt and matching black gun belt strapped to her right leg launched her from his fantasy woman to a real-life contender. He had to meet this woman face-to-face.

"How long?" Kasha asked in clipped tones.

Ice looked at her watch as if mentally calculating and said, "Twelve hours for the first pair. Faster if I can swing it."

Brandon noticed that he, and all the other people in the room, pulled up the dual time function on their watches to add the WAT option. Whether here at the compound or in Africa, it was countdown time when it came to a missing person, especially one known by all.

Kasha looked like she wanted to argue, then conceded quietly.

"In the meantime," Ice said, "gather as much information as you can. Who saw him last? Where? Did he have plans to go anywhere? What is his weapons situation like? Pass it all to Stone and Merk. Understand?"

"Understood." Kasha clicked something in front of her, and the screen went dark.

Levi stepped up beside Ice, their two heads bent in conversation.

Brandon watched the others explain about Bullard to those who weren't in the know. Brandon knew of Bullard but had yet to meet him. And he'd never met Kasha. He'd remember her.

Ice walked out of the room, Levi behind her. Brandon grabbed another cup of coffee and watched to see what, if anything, would come of this. After another hour, he headed to his room.

Levi caught up with him in the hall. "Brandon, in three hours, you're leaving for the airport."

"Where am I going?" he asked, interested to see what his future with the company would hold. He'd been afraid he'd be stuck babysitting stars in California.

"Africa. To find Bullard. And the time frame is yesterday."

And just like that, Levi was gone.

Chapter 1

O N SUNDAY AT 5:30 a.m. CST but 12:30 p.m. per WAT, Brandon cleared security and walked across the tarmac toward the next, much smaller plane. Harrison was at his side. Neither had said a word since arriving in Africa. Brandon had slept on the plane. If he could sleep on those US military cargo carriers, he could sleep anywhere. He presumed Harrison caught some Zs as well. Both knew what needed to be done, and they realized how important the job was. It was even worse that Bullard was the one in trouble. It was always harder when a friend or family member went missing.

With Merk and Stone already over here, Brandon and Harrison knew they'd be met and debriefed as soon as they landed. But, in the meantime, traveling was a bitch.

Before boarding the transatlantic flight, Harrison had brought out his laptop and said, "We'll need to download some information first." He quickly copied files onto a USB key and handed it to Brandon. "Just a little light reading. Make sure you've got it all down before we land."

Once the pilot finally gave the go-ahead to move about the cabin and to use the tray tables, Brandon pulled out his laptop, popped in the USB and opened the files. It was intense reading—a full character workup of all of Bullard's men and Kasha. He learned a lot of the history about

Bullard's group. He read Kasha's background info with interest. She'd been with Bullard for five years and had started in an administrative capacity that had quickly morphed to being Bullard's right-hand man—or woman in this case. Her hobbies were listed as swimming and guns acquisition. As a former SEAL, Brandon had to smile. Yet more they had in common.

At the end was a brief on the issues they currently faced. Brandon had been a part of the initial conference call, so he knew the basics. Outside of some minor details, not much was new. "Bullard had been at the new holding for five days, so are we thinking it's most likely a local job?" Brandon asked.

Harrison shook his head. "It's hard to say. Bullard has connections in the military too, both US and African, so it could be someone who wanted retaliation because Bullard helped take them down or could be some freelancer looking for an opportunity to get control of this area, seeing Bullard as an up-and-coming threat. Also remember Kasha's comment that Bullard had put out the call for new hires at the holding. That was tantamount to broadcasting where he was at that moment to any local mercs."

"Great. He could be in big trouble and with way too many factions possibly looking to take him out."

"Exactly. This trip is all about helping Bullard. He's assisted Ice and Levi many times. He's also the one who helped set up security on the compound. He and Ice go way back. If either puts out a call for help, the other comes running."

"But nobody's heard from Bullard or Kasha since the first transmission?"

"Correct. However, Merk already checked in at both holdings with the help of a helicopter pilot who Ice knew was temporarily in the area. Still no sign of Bullard."

A fact Merk confirmed when Harrison and Brandon arrived at the local airport. Merk talked and walked outside, nodding to the two of them to toss their gear in the back of the jeep before they all climbed in. He didn't say much else, just, "It's about a twenty-five-minute drive. Sit tight. I want to make it in fifteen."

He took off like a race car on a practice run. There was a careless skill in the way he handled the jeep. The roads were rough once they got past the town limits. Then Merk really put his foot to the gas pedal and let the engine rip. He was just past his ETA when they pulled into an estate. It was bigger than Levi's and fancier. Like some ornate European mansion had been transported deep within Africa.

Brandon gave a silent whistle as he hopped out. "Wow, this is something."

Merk nodded. "Bullard has offered to do the same at our place. He says the compound is too ugly for his taste."

Brandon was starting to like Bullard even more. They walked in to find Dave, Bullard's manservant, with his hands clenched tightly together.

Again Merk asked, "No sign of him?"

Dave shook his head.

Merk made the introductions. "Nothing new at all?"

"He was setting up another headquarters," Dave said. "It should have been a simple trip. The property is on the Benin border."

"Are we flying or driving?"

"Flying," Dave said firmly. "No expense will be spared to make sure we find Bullard as expediently as possible."

Just then a woman's voice called out, "Dave, who's here?"

Merk stepped up so the woman could see him. "Hello, Kasha. These are two more of my men. Now we can go."

KASHA LOWRY STUDIED the two new arrivals. She recognized both from the conference call the day before, but neither were men she knew personally. That bothered her. She understood that Levi had thoroughly vetted these men, but had Bullard? Her responsibility was to her missing employer. After working for him for five years, she also considered him a good friend. Her gaze went from Merk to Brandon. At the sight of Brandon, she frowned. "You're late."

Brandon held out his hand. "I'm Brandon. We came as soon as we could. I'm sure we'll find Bullard."

She shook his hand, fear gnawing at her insides. She'd been waiting for these men to show up, Merk and Stone having arrived five hours earlier. "I hope so. It's very unlike Bullard to be silent. We don't have any time to spare." Without waiting for a response, she spun on her heels and walked down a hallway.

Just then Stone called from the other end of it. "Down here, guys."

Kasha led the way to the huge office that was the central hub of Bullard's operation. The medical clinic was attached on the left with its own entrance.

Inside the room Stone greeted the men at Kasha's side while working at the electronics table, building a camera system for the newest holding Bullard had purchased.

"This is Bullard's main office," Kasha explained as she walked over to a computer screen and clicked on several keys, and a big monitor popped to life on the wall. A map filled the screen with a red circle in the center. "This is his last known location."

"Does he have a tracker on?" Brandon asked.

She nodded. "He does. However, it is no longer responding."

"Is it subcutaneous?"

"No, it's hidden in his belt."

The men exchanged glances. Stone's face locked down. "It could be worse. There are many reasons for it to have stopped working."

After that the questions came fast and furious. She answered what she could, but there was damn little anybody on Bullard's team knew. His men, who had accompanied Bullard there, had all gone to look at his new acquisition. They'd been there for five days, making extensive notes of what Bullard wanted done. They had two vehicles delivered and a mess of other deliveries, including food and electronics. Bullard had been busy making plans to develop the property in terms of security. He'd chosen the spot because it was private, and he could build more of the fortress he wanted with less government interference. The property was already halfway there, making it perfect for his needs.

"He wanted a second headquarters, as big as this one," Kasha said. "This will always be his home base because a full medical clinic's here. But he wanted to move some of his military operations away from home into a new location and run the business aspect from over there."

"That's understandable. I'd do the same," Brandon said. "Although I'm not sure I'd want one so far away."

"But the farther away from home meant added safety for those here."

"Makes sense."

Kasha looked around the room. "We have water and a small meal for you to shift gears. We'll be leaving soon, so help yourself."

The others cheered as Dave walked in, pushing a big rolling triple-tiered metal tray full of wraps, sandwiches and what looked like hand-size meat pies.

Brandon asked, "Bathroom?"

She pointed to a small door off to the side. "Down there."

He headed for it as she watched with her peripheral vision until he closed the door. Then she turned to Merk who was eyeing the meat pies. "Help yourself. We'll be flying out in twenty minutes."

"Everything packed and ready?"

She nodded. "We've just been waiting for your team's arrival."

He couldn't seem to decide what to choose and ended up taking two meat pies. The first one went down in just a couple bites. The second he savored, even as he picked up a third.

She laughed. "Good, aren't they?"

"Delicious," he muttered with a full mouth.

Stone had no trouble picking and choosing, taking his plate back to the work bench.

"Where is the airport?" Harrison asked from behind her.

She turned slightly to speak to both men, pointing to another monitor trained on this holding.

Brandon stepped out of the bathroom in time to catch her response. He snagged a meat pie as he listened.

"I have a helicopter warming up. There's no time to waste. We'd have used the helicopter to bring you back to the house, but your arrival times differed every time I checked the airport's ETAs."

Brandon looked at her in surprise and then whispered to Merk, "Too bad Ice isn't here."

"Or the guy who heloed me about earlier before he had to leave. It took longer but got the job done," Merk added. "Bullard is a hell of a pilot himself." Merk shook his head. "Bullard always had more money than we did. Knowing him, this helo will be one of the latest and the best. Ice would love to be flying one of those."

"So true," Kasha said with a wry smile. "I love that about her. Ice was always the first to jump in and fly to the rescue." She'd heard lots of stories from Bullard about Ice. Plus she and Levi had been to Africa both to visit and for business meetings several times, so Kasha had met them personally. Bullard called them family. Kasha wasn't as close to them as he was, but it was a nice concept.

They needed to get moving. She had everyone outside and loaded up within minutes. With everyone in place, they lifted off. She loved to fly in the helicopter. Bullard spared no expense in his working life.

They had barely been airborne when they landed at the airport where they transferred to a small plane. Brandon leaned forward to Merk and asked, "Is this his private airstrip?"

Merk nodded. "It is indeed."

"We gotta get us one of these."

Merk just chuckled.

The transfer was made very quickly. Their pilot got out of the helicopter and moved into the plane, taking the pilot's seat. Flying the two involved very different skill sets, but it seemed that, in this world, everybody had multiple talents. And they were damn good at each of them.

The plane ride was just over an hour. When they landed, nobody came to greet them. Also no vehicle waited for them at the secondary holding.

The pilot hopped out with them and said, "I'll be back tomorrow morning at 8:00 a.m. Gives you twenty-four hours." He glared at them all. "Be here with Bullard."

Chapter 2

THEY WAITED UNTIL he'd gone and then turned and headed to Bullard's newest holding. The airstrip was on a plateau of land that overlooked the holding below. It was an impressive sight with the perimeter walls made out of stone and the huge building rising in the center.

"Looks like a medieval castle amid a small walled city," Brandon said.

Kasha nodded, then laughed. "Despite its appearance, this construction is more recent than that. Still we could not find blueprints for the buildings here. Seems the local townships don't keep up with those documents in every instance." She glanced around them at their surroundings and continued, "The central edifice is five stories tall, with Bullard's main control room set up on the first floor, along with a working kitchen and an impromptu ER. That was the last update I received from Bullard before he went missing. There is an underground garage that has a secret exit at the back of the residence at the perimeter wall and one public entryway through electronic gates to get past the wall. The upper four floors are mostly large rooms meant for living areas or bedrooms. I don't know the extent of Bullard's plans for their renovation."

Once again Kasha led the way toward the buildings. She stiffened, sensing eyes on them. She knew the others would have felt the same thing. They had no idea what might be waiting for them. The area was flat, covered with sparse vegetation and dotted with trees in an otherwise sand-and-dirt landscape for miles.

Brandon stepped forward and asked, "Do you have this place under observation?"

"No," she said quietly. "That's not us."

As she approached the perimeter wall, instead of heading to the main entrance, Kasha unlocked a side door that led inside the massive stone wall to a four-foot-wide passageway. She'd loved the wall the first time she'd seen it. The wall enclosed the entire development and yard, even rising over the driveway and gates in a continuous circle, with a rampart along the top of the wall, which made for a defense system not seen since the Middle Ages.

As they walked through, she could look inside and out of the property through small openings in the wall. She could hear the men murmuring in the background. She knew how they felt. This place was fabulous and just what Bullard wanted. Of course, being in the same industry, the men accompanying her would recognize the benefits of such architecture.

When they came to the next corner, she unlocked and pulled open a small door and entered a partially stocked weapons room. "Well, that's a good sign." She was quietly relieved the weapons were here. She had to admit to being afraid the place had been broken into and cleaned out. Over one million dollars' worth of Bullard's equipment, weapons and vehicles were here.

"Oh, now that's more like it," Brandon said with a big grin. "Wow. Okay, I wasn't expecting this."

She chuckled. *Follow your bliss* came to mind. Like boys

in a candy shop, each exclaimed and chose their favorite weapons. She watched as Brandon grabbed a handgun, which he tucked into his waistband. He then selected a semiautomatic rifle.

As he stepped back, she pointed to the far wall. He looked up to see belt clips full of ammo. He took one, strapped it on and followed her out. She was also armed but her choice was two pistols.

Kasha walked forward confidently. She opened the double doors into the main area of the property, wondering what she'd find left here. So far there was no sign the place had been broken into. "This main residence is huge. I'm heading to the heart of the building on the main floor." She led the way to the huge central room equipped with large-screen monitors, TVs, speakers, desks. "This is where we started setting up a command station."

Brandon stood in the entranceway and whistled quietly. "Wow. *This* is a war room."

The others looked at him and nodded. "They aren't all that uncommon over here," Stone commented. "At least for any kind of military operation. It'll be awesome when it's finished."

Kasha walked over to the computers. The big wall screen behind her showed her logging in. Within seconds, a hand-drawn plan for each floor popped up on the big screen. "Like I said earlier, no such things as blueprints were available regarding this property. So Bullard drew these up himself, and I uploaded them."

Brandon walked closer, the others following suit. He asked, "Is this just the house we're in?"

"Yes. All five floors."

"Do we have any idea where Bullard could be? Maybe

even in this main building?"

She tapped two more buttons, and three red dots appeared on the third floor. "Heat sensors," she said quietly.

"Too small," Brandon said, shaking his head.

She gave him a sharp look. "What do you mean?"

"None are big enough to be Bullard," Merk said. "Were there any dogs here?"

Kasha shrugged. "Not that I know of."

"Stone and Harrison will stay here with you, Kasha," Merk said. "Harrison is our resident IT expert and hacker, so put him to use as you see fit. And, as you already know, Stone is our mechanical engineer who can create whatever you want from just an idea. If you do have dogs or other animals to deal with, Flynn's your man, but he's not here, although he could be called in at any time."

"Great," she said. "Bullard's security is not yet fully operational. Stone, Harrison and I will see what's been done and what we can do to improve on that."

"And the two of us will check out those heat signatures," Merk said. "Brandon, with me."

She frowned. "Be careful," she warned.

Brandon gave her a ferocious grin. "We will. We'll also find out who is here."

Merk and Brandon grabbed comm units, linking them to the command center, as Brandon spoke to Kasha on his way out. "There were two sets of stairs—one on either side of the building—yet the elevator goes literally up the center. Is that correct?"

Kasha nodded and said, "I disengaged the elevator before I left here, under Bullard's orders. He prefers to take the stairs anyway. The house is built around this main core, a square within the larger square. All the main floor functions are centralized here, and outside of this are extra rooms. Above are more living areas. Lots of places to hide. And it's been unoccupied for the better part of two days now."

On the active screen in the war room, she watched as the red dots representing Merk and Brandon climbed the stairs to the third floor. Once there, they searched each room, stating, "Clear," as they moved from one room to the other.

She watched their progress with awe. They were like a well-oiled machine.

Until they walked past where the first heat signature was.

"Stop," she said urgently. "You just passed one."

"Shit."

She guided them as they retraced their steps into the last room. "Check at the very back on the left," she murmured.

They walked over to the wall where a small built-in closet was. She heard Brandon call out, "We're opening the door. We're armed and prepared to shoot."

"Come out or be shot," Merk added, before he yanked open the door.

She could see the first red dot stretch up.

"Kasha, we found an older woman here," Brandon said quietly. "She looks pretty terrified."

In her headset, Kasha could hear him ask, "Do you speak English?"

"It could be the cook," Kasha said. "Ask if her name is Tahlia."

As soon as Brandon mentioned the name, the woman spoke in a rapid-fire language and tone Kasha recognized. "I think it's the cook Bullard hired from the village. Once you've completed your sweep, bring her down here."

"So where's the next heat signature?" Brandon asked.

"Go east. Far back corner of that floor. Should be another closet or a small room." She waited for their next communication and then jumped when she heard the resounding gunshot. "What did you find?"

"A black mamba," Brandon said.

"I hate snakes. It's one of the worst things about living in Africa."

"Yeah, well, you would have really disliked this one," Merk said and then laughed.

"Why is that?" Kasha asked.

"This one is a granddaddy. I bet it's ten feet long when stretched out."

"Thanks for killing that one. Now I'll be scared to open any door in this place."

"Always a good idea to call in an exterminator with each new property," Brandon said. "I've stayed in some supposed safe houses that weren't so healthy for its occupants. That wouldn't happen with any of Levi's safe houses. He knows better."

"Okay, where's the last heat signature?" Merk asked.

"Uh-oh," Kasha said. "It's on the move. Heading toward you. Should have a visual in three, two …"

"Got it. Some starving wild dog," Merk said.

Kasha could hear it growling over the guys' comms. "Probably what the locals call a village dog. They're feral guard dogs, very territorial, so beware, guys," Kasha said.

"I've got an idea, Merk." Brandon nodded toward their fresh kill behind them. "I think the dog wants raw meat. Let him pass and take care of our dead friend back there."

Kasha held her breath as she heard their softened footfalls, then got another "Clear" from Brandon. "I've closed the dog up in this room. We'll have to deal with him later, hopefully when his stomach is full."

The men arrived back in the war room within minutes, ushering Tahlia in front of them.

Kasha walked over, smiling at the cringing woman. Kasha spoke quickly, trying to reassure her that she wasn't in any danger.

The other woman relaxed, and her tone changed as she spoke with Kasha.

Kasha listened, then turned to the men who awaited an explanation. "Bullard hired her to cook for us while we were here with an eye to a permanent full-time position down the road as soon as he set up the place."

At that, they asked several questions, with Kasha translating, but the cook's answers were not helpful. "Bullard left, saying he'd be back before lunch, but he didn't return. She didn't know what to do but wait. She doesn't understand computers and has no cell phone to call anyone. She doesn't know what happened to him."

"Do we believe her?" Brandon asked, careful to keep his voice neutral. "It wouldn't be the first time somebody lied in a situation like this."

"True enough," Kasha said quietly. "But I believe her. At least that she's telling the truth as she knows it."

"Okay, so where do we go from here?" They turned to look at the rest of the building. "Did the heat sensors pick anything else up?"

Kasha shook her head. "No, not that I could see. Remember, it's not decked out Bullard-style yet as he just took possession of the property. That's part of what he was doing after we left him."

"And he didn't call afterward?"

She nodded. "He didn't call, and we've had no contact since. If our men weren't all over the world on missions, we'd have had the personnel to take care of this. But Dave suggested someone outside this situation was better than pulling our men back. The only people Bullard trusts are Levi and Ice." She added, "We need to check outside that he's not lying somewhere on the property, hurt or disabled. Although the sensors we have installed so far should have picked that up. Still, we need to do a walk around."

"Got a preview for us?" Stone asked, pointing to the computers.

She shook her head. "So far we've got limited cameras on the surrounding property, like at the garage, but not on the gate yet. There's a rooftop walkway all around the top of this building—the proverbial widow's walk—which should give you a bird's-eye view before hiking across the actual property. As you've seen firsthand, the property is exposed. But, up there, you are somewhat shielded by a chest-high parapet with gun ports at various points in the wall."

Pairing up in twos, with Kasha and the cook staying at the computer center, Brandon and Merk took the left staircase, and Stone and Harrison went to the right one. Both would end up at the rooftop walkway.

They had a fifteen-minute rendezvous time as the four men checked all the floors in the building. They started on the first floor and moved up each of the five floors before stepping out onto the turret wall. Aside from the Bullard-approved enhancements made to the ground floor, all the others held sparse furniture and were replicas of the ones before it with stone walls and brick floors to mimic ancient structures. However, contemporary glass windows all throughout helped to keep the African heat at bay.

"Stepping outside now. Clear so far."

She smiled at Brandon's voice. Something was very

magnetic about it. If he sang, he'd be a bass—it was that low. With their shared comm system, she could hear the guys talking through her headset.

"This rooftop walkway is incredible," Brandon said to Merk. "The layout is from castle-sieging days. I can see why Bullard wanted it."

There was a crackle in the headset. "We can't see the plateau where the airstrip is," Merk said. "That's a definite weakness in the system."

"Bullard did note that on our original walk-through," Kasha pointed out. "We added it to the lists of problems to address."

Stone called through at one point and asked, "Anything?"

Merk answered, "No, nothing. You?"

"Clear here," Stone said.

"Clear," Harrison added.

"Roof is clear," Brandon said. "It's a flat spot that's great for a lookout. The view is stunning. Can see any enemy coming from miles away."

"Heading down to the grounds," Merk said.

Keeping an eye on them, she followed the corresponding red dots revealed on the war room screen as the guys circled the building. They continued through the courtyard and around the main house, checking into the few outbuildings as well. They were small and didn't take much time to investigate.

As soon as they returned to the war room, she flashed a smile. "I suggest someone check out the garage too." She motioned for the four guys to follow her as she led the way to the underground six-car garage. Out of the corner of her eye she saw the cook sticking close to them. When they reached the garage, Kasha eyed the two vehicles there. She tapped the concrete floor with her foot.

"What's up?" Brandon asked.

She shook her head as she looked at the vehicles and said, "Bullard must be driving the old pickup truck that came with this place."

Merk asked, "Is the pickup being tracked?"

Kasha's brows rose in startled surprise, and she nodded. "Yes, it should be. Let's check the system. The men installed trackers right away—or were supposed to—but tons of things were to be done, and we were missing some of the tools and equipment they needed. However, if the job was completed, chances are good no one would suspect a GPS unit in that old clunker."

She opened a nearby floor-to-ceiling cabinet, exposing a computer center, and clicked on the garage's keyboard unit. "Got it," she cried out. She pointed to the screen behind her mounted to the wall that just blinked on. And sure enough a buzzing red dot flashed on the screen.

The cook spoke up then. She pointed to the screen, and her voice became animated.

Kasha listened carefully, then translated. "That's the closest village. She said a lot of really bad men live there."

"That's fine. They're about to meet us, and we'll winnow them down," Brandon said in a harsh voice. He checked his watch. "10:05 a.m. WAT." He turned his attention to Kasha and asked, "Which vehicle do you want us to take?"

She smiled and said, "The Hummer." She walked to a cabinet equipped with a digital lock. She punched in a series of numbers and opened it to show a row of keys. She pulled out two sets and double-checked them. "You drive."

Like a kid with a new toy, Brandon whooped. He and

the other men raced to the Hummer as Kasha walked to a control panel on the side on the wall. She clicked several buttons, and they watched as the huge garage door opened, revealing a large ramp up and out of the building.

She said, "I'm staying behind, in case you need anything further, in case Bullard shows up, and in case of any more surprises."

Merk snapped his head to Stone.

Stone hopped out, slapped the Hummer twice in code and said, "Go. I've got it."

BRANDON DIDN'T ARGUE. He hit Reverse, backed down the large ramp and turned around.

He could see Stone and Kasha arguing in his rearview mirror. Given the circumstances, he fully agreed with Stone staying back. The last sight he saw was Stone crossing his arms over his chest and just staring at Kasha.

Brandon chuckled. "I don't think she liked that much."

"It doesn't matter if she liked it or not," Merk said. "There's no way we come here to rescue Bullard and get Kasha kidnapped or killed in the process."

"Keep in mind we don't know how many men we'll be up against in the village," Harrison commented.

"And keep in mind Kasha has weapons training. Bullard trained her himself," Merk said. "He wanted to ensure she could handle herself when he was away. I know he was contemplating basing her here, but she didn't want to come this far out."

"I heard she was looking to head back to the US again," Harrison said.

"Have you guys worked with her before?" Brandon

asked.

"A couple times. She's good people." Merk held up a cell phone. "The GPS is showing the tracker on the missing vehicle."

"Good. What a world we live in where everything can be reduced to a screenshot on a phone held in our hands."

"It could be that Bullard was taken and even killed for the vehicle. In this area, that relic of a pickup still runs and is worth gold to them, whether they keep it or intend to sell it," Harrison noted. "Whoever has the truck may not want to give it up either."

"I don't give a shit what they would like," Brandon said quietly. "That vehicle comes back with us. That's the only evidence we have that Bullard was here. We can't take a chance of losing that too."

"What if Bullard sold it to them?" Harrison asked.

"Then they can take it up with him when he's back on his feet. In the meantime, we treat them all as if they are against him," Merk said.

"Well then, we'd better find him. No way will I face his team or ours and tell them we failed," Brandon added.

Just before they entered town, Brandon could see buildings lining either side of the road. Businesses of some sort. Houses seemed to sit behind the business row but not many. A rise was off to the left. He drove the vehicle to the top, and they hopped out and walked over to the edge to look down on the village. With little to impede their view, it was easy to see Bullard's vehicle, parked between two houses off the main road. They snuck down the hill on foot and around the back of the houses, then took another couple minutes to work their way around to where the vehicle was.

Brandon had the spare keys in his pocket. What they

really wanted was to know what happened to the driver. Merk gave a signal that he was going on ahead with Harrison giving him backup. Brandon snuck around to come up behind the vehicle. He was at the passenger side as he caught sight of a clipboard on the front seat. It had BULL emblazoned on the front. Such a Bullard attitude. Brandon checked underneath and in the back but couldn't see anything suspicious or noteworthy.

A small adobe hovel was on the right. Crossing over, Brandon sent a short Morse code message via his comm before he slipped inside to find it empty and cold. Nobody had used this place for days if not weeks. Creeping back outside, he crossed to the building on the other side and found the same thing. All the buildings at this end of the village appeared to be deserted. They were in rough condition, but it was interesting that the truck was here. Was the whole village involved or just one or two bad apples? The latter was more likely.

Back outside the other two waited for him. He walked up, motioning to both houses and whispered, "Both clear."

They nodded, and the three spread out, sticking close, and went on a house-by-house search. Harrison served as a lookout to the rear, while Brandon went inside each one, leaving Merk as the scout going ahead to the next target. There was no sign of anybody for several more houses, but, as they came closer to the main part of town, they could hear English-speaking voices.

"We can't just keep him here."

"I say, kill him."

"You know that'll just bring more problems down on our heads," another man snapped. "The others don't deserve that."

"It's Bullard. If we don't kill him, this won't end here and now."

"He's almost dead anyway. What difference does it make?"

"It matters," protested the first man. "If we take him back now, he'll forgive us. I, and some of the others, didn't know what we were getting into."

"Well, you're in the middle of it now."

"We had nothing to do with his kidnapping."

Merk, Harrison and Brandon listened, trying to get as much information as they could.

"Bullard won't believe that."

Merk motioned with his head, and they quickly surrounded the house and stepped in both doors at the same time, guns at the ready. They faced a table of six men; two were white men, and four were locals, each fully armed but caught unaware. Nobody had time to draw his weapon. The oldest of the white men stood. He lifted his hands and asked, "Are you here for Bullard?"

Merk nodded.

The man pointed behind them to where Bullard lay against the wall, out cold. Brandon holstered his weapon and checked Bullard's pulse. "He's alive."

"Yes, he is, but he's in bad shape."

"Why didn't you get him help?" Merk asked. "Was it your job to kill him?"

The man shook his head rapidly. "No. We happened upon him already unconscious in his truck. We knew what was happening at the walled-in place, but we didn't realize how bad it would get. We had heard rumors, but we didn't realize it involved Bullard."

"How the hell do you know who Bullard is?"

"It's one of the reasons we're here. We were hoping to get hired on. We heard he was looking for men."

"And you expect him to hire you now that we find out you were part of his kidnapping?"

"But we weren't," the older man said. "I'm Peter. We don't know what's going on."

"Yet you didn't contact his local headquarters?"

"We did, but nobody was there," the younger man said in protest. He also stood with his hands up to make sure everyone could see they were empty. "We would never have done that to him. We're seriously looking for work. He put the word out that he was looking for good men."

Brandon looked at him hard. "Military?"

The man nodded. "I've been a mercenary for the last six years. It's not exactly my preferred choice, but I was hoping to work for Bullard. I've heard a lot of good things about him," he admitted.

Brandon didn't trust any of them. He said, "We'll be taking Bullard and his vehicle with us."

"Can we help you carry him?" one of the men asked eagerly.

Merk shook his head. "But we'll take his belongings that you stole."

The men looked at Merk in surprise, then looked at each other. The older one said, "That just might be a little harder to do." His smile indicated he wouldn't be returning anything.

"No, it won't be," Brandon snapped. "You said you're on Bullard's side, and you want to work for him. He won't tolerate anybody who steals from him, regardless if you kidnapped him or not."

As far as Brandon could see, this group was a mix of ex-military, possibly looking at Bullard for a source of work, and the locals could have seen Bullard as a boon to their economy. But then who the hell had kidnapped him?

Peter waved at the locals and said, "They want something in return for storing his vehicle."

"The fact they're not wearing my bullets right now is a sign of my goodwill," Merk said in a hard voice. "We find you all in possession of the kidnapped man who is injured, and you haven't done anything to get him medical attention."

"Just so you know that we had nothing to do with his kidnapping," Peter snapped, "we found him in his vehicle and didn't know what to do. A large militant group occupied that holding he bought. I think they were the ones who went after him."

"And why would they do that?"

Peter shrugged. "I don't know. They have lived here for the last year off and on. I don't think they liked the idea of Bullard taking over their base. Then again there were rumors," he admitted, "that they were involved in illegal activities. So they might want the base back."

"Well, they won't be getting it now. Hand over all of Bullard's belongings, and then we'll leave."

One of the group made a move for a gun. The single shot fired sent everybody seeking cover except for the man screaming on the floor.

Brandon looked over at Harrison. "Good shot." While the rest of the villagers were stunned, staring at the guy's blood that had sprayed everywhere, Brandon stealthily took pictures of them with his cell.

Harrison nodded grimly and spoke to the villagers again. "That was the one and only freebie. I only took out his hand raising the weapon. The next man who raises a weapon against us won't get the same courtesy."

Within minutes, they had Bullard loaded up in the middle of the cab of his truck with his weapons, ammo, wallet, cell phone, the elusive belt with the incapacitated GPS and his laptop. Merk held Bullard steady to keep him from rocking too much on the bench seat, while Brandon sat in the driver's seat, with Harrison riding in the bed. They drove to where they'd parked the Hummer. There Brandon hopped into the second vehicle, Harrison taking over driving the truck, and they all headed back to the holding.

The man they'd shot would need medical attention, but Brandon figured he'd get it faster than they gave Bullard any. Which was a damn shame because Bullard could have employed most of them—but not any longer. He'd never trust any of the men involved in this botched-up kidnapping. The drive back was short and hard. Brandon wasn't sure they could trust any of the men they'd left behind, so he kept an eye out for anybody following them, keeping the Hummer at least a full minute behind Bullard's truck.

Brandon could see the geography, open and flat, which gave him visibility for a long way. A militant group living in the empty holding for any length of time wasn't good news. Although they wouldn't likely attack the holding now, knowing many more men were there to defend it. Men not afraid to shoot them, if need be. As Brandon and his team had just proven in the village.

But their priority was getting the entire group back to Bullard's main holding, the mansion Bullard called home.

That would be hours away as it was only noon now. They had to make it through the night before the airplane came to fly them back at eight in the morning. Brandon was damn sure, if they wanted to do a midnight flight, that was possible, but for some reason they'd been left for a whole day to get the job done. He'd figured four hours would have done it, and he was right. But it was a bit of a fluke they'd found Bullard in the first place. The trouble was getting him the medical attention he needed since they were stranded in this unpopulated area in a temporary holding not fully outfitted yet for another twenty hours.

Bullard *was* the doctor here. Brandon didn't know if anybody else was qualified to help. All Levi's men were good at rough-and-ready field medicine, but, if you needed more than that, it wasn't to be had as Ice was their medic.

Kasha must have been watching the computer monitors as the garage door raised just in time for Levi's team to drive Bullard's truck and the Hummer into the downstairs garage. The doors closed quickly behind them.

As he pulled up and parked to the left of Bullard's old truck, Brandon could see Kasha and Tahlia had already surrounded Bullard. Kasha had brought a gurney on wheels.

The men quickly transferred Bullard onto the gurney and wheeled it into the room adjoining the main computer area. Kasha pushed it farther into the room toward a desk with some medical equipment. Brandon walked up and studied Kasha. "Are you a doctor too?"

She snorted. "No, the doctor is the one lying on the table. I've helped him out on a few occasions. But I'm certainly not qualified for anything major. We need to get him back to the main estate for that. That's where all the real equipment is."

"Can you send a request for the plane to come now?" Merk asked. "That's when we need it. Not tomorrow morning."

She shook her head. "I don't think they will come. We've set up the flight for eight."

"Bullard needs attention now. Not eight in the morning," Brandon said flatly. "What kind of an outfit are they that they can't come and get the boss?"

Kasha shot him a hard glance. "Don't judge what you don't know."

He shrugged. "Loyalty has to mean more than just following orders blindly." He knew there was bitterness in his tone, but it was hard not to feel that way after what he'd been through. He didn't talk about it though. One had to make a stand at some point in one's life. He'd made his. Hence, being private now instead of in the military.

Her gaze searched his, but she never asked the question. She cut away Bullard's shirt as Stone checked his head. "We've definitely got a concussion," Stone announced. "He'll need stitches on the side of his skull here too."

Bullard hadn't made a sound so far. His body temperature was dropping, and his skin showed signs of a chill.

Brandon looked inside all the cabinets. "Where will I find blankets?" he asked.

Kasha spoke a bit of whatever foreign language the cook spoke, then Kasha told Brandon, "Follow her. She'll lead you to where the bed linens are."

He glanced around the room and said, "Nothing's down here?"

Kasha turned her attention back to Bullard. She continued to cut as she answered Brandon. "No, they're still all up on the next floor."

"What's the cook's name again?" he asked.

"Tahlia," Kasha said. "At least that's the easiest form for you to pronounce."

He followed the cook, not at all sure he trusted her. But she was a whole lot smaller than he was and at least thirty years older and didn't appear to carry any weapons. But he'd seen odder scenarios in his life. He stayed back a few steps as Tahlia ambled forward. When she led him to a big double closet in one of the halls, it was indeed full of bedding. On the bottom were blankets. He grabbed three, nodded his thanks and raced back downstairs again.

He waited for Kasha to finish checking Bullard's chest. "You're taking his pants off too? He's already chilled."

"I already did a full check on the lower half of his body," Stone said. "I'm not seeing any more injuries."

"The main injury is his head? How bad?" Kasha asked.

"The main physical trauma is to his head. It doesn't appear to be that bad."

Kasha stepped away and glanced at Bullard and then to the monitors. "I'm also worried about drugs."

Stone shrugged. "It's not necessarily bad drugs. They may have given him something for the pain, or they may have given him something to sedate him while they figured out what to do with him."

As soon as they all stepped back, Brandon bundled up Bullard with several blankets. He wrapped one around his feet where his toes already were bluish. "I wonder how long he's been like this."

"It's hard to say," Stone replied. "At least one full day. He hasn't been missing that long. His knuckles are scraped up and battered as if he put up a good fight somewhere along the line."

"They likely smashed him over the head to initially subdue him," Kasha said. "Still, it's better than popping him with a couple bullets. I hear you shot somebody in town,

Brandon."

"Not me," he said cheerfully. "That was Harrison. But I would have. I've got no issue with those types of men."

"What? Honest upright citizens trying to make a living?" she asked in a mocking tone.

He snorted. "Mercs. They all have their uses, and maybe they'll be good and loyal eventually. But right now they're slimy. I'd advise Bullard to not hire any of them."

"Do you have anything other than personal prejudice for that reasoning?"

"Yeah, they didn't look after their goddamn guns."

The other men stopped to look down at theirs.

Brandon shrugged. "Did you see them?"

The men shook their heads.

"You can always tell what kind of a man he is by the condition of the weapons he keeps." He caught the other two staring at each other and glancing over at Kasha. But he ignored them. He reached down and checked Bullard's pulse. It was strong and steady. "Given the sheer laxity and paleness of his skin," he said, "I'm going with a knockout drug." He turned to find Kasha bringing out a syringe and staring at it. "Probably gamma-hydroxybutyric acid, or date rape drug and common all over the world. He'll come out of this without any side effects just fine."

"I don't have any of the necessary equipment here, but, as soon as we get home, I can get it tested."

"If we won't be home for at least twenty hours, the date rape drug won't be detectable. It's already leaving the body at eight hours and completely gone by twelve," he said gently. "Better to pull the blood when we get there. Except that the drugs may have worked through his system by then too."

Merk stepped forward. "Kasha, are you sure we can't get

the pilot here sooner?"

She looked up at him steadily and said, "I'm under orders not to call them."

The men's eyebrows rose. "Whose orders?"

"Bullard's."

Chapter 3

K ASHA STARED AT the men defiantly. She knew they didn't understand. She wasn't even sure *she* understood. Bullard's instructions had been clear. She was to follow the time schedule as laid out and to not deviate. No matter what happened. She'd protested in the past, saying sometimes things happened on the fly, and plans needed to be adjusted, but Bullard had been adamant. *No. Stick to the schedule. Everything will work out.*

She stared down at her unconscious boss. "But it's not fine, dammit."

"What's not fine?"

She looked up to see the men staring at her, their gazes hard and clearly not understanding why she wasn't calling in the emergency ranks. She quickly explained Bullard's instructions.

Merk crossed his arms over his chest. "I've known Bullard a long time. He always has a reason for everything he does."

She nodded. "He does. But I don't know if he would consider these current circumstances enough to warrant a change now."

Merk excused himself to take a lookout position on the rooftop walkway. He took Harrison with him, both of them taking a comm unit with them.

Brandon and Stone stood beside her, watching her. She tried to ignore them as she cleaned off Bullard's face and chest. He did look drugged. His cheeks sagged, and his neck was nowhere near the same thick imposing firmness like when he was upright. Something was off. She'd already run as many tests as she could and had written down the stats. She had already spoken with Levi and Ice, had a call in to Dave. She could only do so much. She checked her watch and said, "Nineteen hours. We only have to wait nineteen more hours."

But before they said a word, she already knew what they would say. *Bullard might not have nineteen hours.* Then her phone rang, and she smiled as she donned her headset and hooked up the caller to the wall screen for a conference call. "Dave, we found him."

Dave's relief came through with a shout of joy. "How is he?"

"He's unconscious. We found a head injury, but we're not seeing much else." She explained where Bullard had been found.

"I told him not to put out the word he was looking to hire local help. That's never a good thing. It brings all the scum out of the woodwork. You'll never figure out which ones are good and which ones aren't."

"I know," Kasha said. "The other thing is, the pilot said he will be back at 8:00 a.m. And we're worried because we think Bullard's been drugged."

"Right, Bullard and his bloody schedules. He said we weren't allowed to deviate from them."

"So he told you that too?" she asked in relief.

He nodded. "Yes, he always does. But we must make decisions sometimes that go against what he wants. He might be angry when he wakes up, but that's a whole lot better than him not waking up at all because we didn't call for help."

"So what should I do?" she asked.

"What do the men think?"

Brandon stepped forward so Dave could see him on the screen. "Hi, Dave. Brandon here. As far as I can see, Bullard's got a head injury, and they've given him drugs to keep him sedated. I don't know if they were painkillers or just knockout drugs or worse. His pulse is strong and steady. However, he needs to sleep off the drugs or purge them from his system."

"The head injury is not as easy to write off," Stone said. "It would be nice if we had an X-ray machine to see if he's got a skull fracture or concussion. As you well know, a bleed on the brain is very serious."

Dave's expression became worried. "Yes, indeed. Brain bleeds are the worst. I'm not sure we should fly him anywhere because of that possibility."

Brandon had to consider that. "We're not going very high in altitude. So I don't think," he said cautiously, "that should be a problem."

"But we don't know that, do we? If Bullard's sleeping it off, and there's no change in his condition, I suggest we leave him where he is. Keep an eye on him, set up an IV and get fluids flowing through his system to flush out those drugs."

"There aren't any such supplies here," Kasha said. "I've been looking." She turned to look around in the cabinets. "I'll give this place another good once-over, but we haven't been here long enough to stock up the medical bay."

"Of course it doesn't come with a standard first aid kit." Dave ran fingers through his hair and said, "Short of having activated charcoal about, I can think of two homeopathic solutions. Why not immerse him in a coffee bath? Surely coffee is there. That's supposed to pull out toxins, even drugs. If not coffee, look for Epsom salts. If Bullard's running a fever, put him in a cool-water bath. If he's chilled, make it a warm-water solution."

"We'll try that. A warm bath will heat him up even if we find no Epsom salts and drink our coffee instead," Kasha said.

"I'll call you back in about an hour. Let me know if there's a change in his condition before then." He clicked off, and the screen went blank.

Kasha looked to Brandon and said, "Why don't you give me a hand, and we'll go through each cabinet down here." She added, "Bullard thought there might be squatters on the property as we found a lot of household stuff when we first arrived. I don't know what we might find now."

Stone stepped forward and said, "You guys check the left. I'll check the right."

Splitting up, they carefully went through each of the cabinets. This medic station was lined in them. With the cook sitting patiently beside Bullard and with Brandon following her, Kasha moved steadily down the wall. "There's everything in here but medical equipment."

"Which is to be expected. It all should be in one spot, wherever it is." He pulled out several fire extinguishers, checked the dates, realized they were well past the use-by date—as in over ten years ago—and put them back in the cabinet with a frown. "I know this building resembles something from the days of castles and moats, but exactly how old is this property, and how long was it left empty?"

"This main building is over eighty years old," she said.

"They don't build them like this anymore. It was supposedly empty for over five years, when the former owner died and had no family to pass this down to, but, as you can see, it has signs of being recently inhabited." She kept moving down the cabinets. She found everything from weapons and gun cleaning supplies to more equipment to create and build their own ammo. Everything but the needed medical supplies. She turned to Brandon who was still at the cabinet full of ammunition-making equipment.

She asked, "Why are you so fascinated with this?"

"I'm always interested in things that go boom in the night," he half joked.

They continued through the rest of the cabinets until they had searched the entire ER room. The room itself was way bigger than the main floor of most houses. In fact, it was bigger than a six-car garage. He shook his head. "It's massive down here."

She nodded. "It's one of the reasons Bullard really loved this place. He said this floor alone had so much potential as a war room and command central, and he wanted to set it up right."

"I can see that. But he forgot to clean out the human snake pit first."

She laughed. "Bullard lives for those kinds of snakes, remember?"

Brandon looked at her and smiled.

It was one of the first natural smiles she'd seen out of him. So far, he'd been edgy and hard, almost angry. But now he was laughing, joking and carefree. It looked good on him. She smiled back and said, "There's a room over here. Let's check it out."

She led the way. As soon as she opened the door, she

heard the spit—a gun with a silencer—but had no time to react. Brandon tossed her to the ground, a hand beneath her head to protect it. Even as he landed beside her, Brandon was already rolling and firing. She knew the others would hear their defending gunfire as none of them were using silencers. She had pulled out both her guns but couldn't see anything. What the hell just happened? This interior side room was used for storage.

She scrambled to her feet and crept along the outer edge of the room. She didn't dare call out. When she heard another spit, she flattened to the floor again.

That spit was followed by several other hard spits and then a grunt. She knew somebody was hit. She stayed where she was, the darkness all encompassing. As her eyes adjusted, she saw Brandon detach himself from the shadows and slip around the corner.

"All clear," he called out. "He's down."

She raced to his side. "Can you see who it is?" she asked.

He pulled out his cell phone and turned on the flashlight, holding it to the side of the man's face. As the light shone, she could hear Stone's running footsteps. "It's okay," she called out both on her headset to notify Merk and Harrison and loud enough for Stone to hear her. "Brandon got him."

Stone stopped when he saw the man on the floor. "Did you kill him?"

Brandon looked up and nodded. "Sorry."

"Too bad. If we'd had him alive, we could have questioned him."

Kasha's hand when to her headset. "Merk's coming. Harrison's staying on point."

They all stared down at the white man. He was dressed

like a soldier, in fatigues and camouflage gear.

Brandon bent down and searched his pockets. He pulled out a wallet and tossed it to Stone and then checked through the rest of his pockets. "I sure hope he wasn't active military. This had better not be an operation we stepped into," Brandon snapped.

"No, it isn't," Harrison said. "There's no name on the fatigues, and the styling's old. This is Army Surplus–looking stuff. He might have been military at one time. But he's likely a merc now."

Nothing else was in his pockets except a lighter and a couple coins and three keys. Brandon didn't know what the keys were for, but he dumped them into Stone's hand before heading for the dead man's boots. He took them off and searched the inside, one by one.

Kasha watched him curiously. "Why the boots?"

"Because a lot of men on missions keep a photograph or a letter from their loved ones there. It's for good luck," he said shortly.

She hadn't heard that before. It was fascinating to consider. In this case, the man didn't have anything in his boots. But when Brandon pulled off one sock, sure enough a simple piece of paper fell out. She picked it up and opened it. "It's got Bullard's name on it and the address. Well, rather the location. It's not like there's an address here."

The piece of paper was handed around, but there was nothing else helpful to be gained from it.

"Even with fingerprints, these freelance merc types wouldn't be in anybody's database when they're working small villages and abandoned properties, like this guy was. He's way too small potatoes and under the radar," Brandon said as he pulled off the other sock. When he found nothing, he put both socks back on and then slid the boots atop.

Again she couldn't help asking, "Why are you putting his boots back on?"

"He died the way he lived," Brandon said, his voice curt. "He was a soldier, one way or another, and they like to die with their boots on."

She stepped back, understanding it was a code among soldiers, but to her it made more sense to take off the boots. The man would be heavy enough without putting those things on him as well. But when Brandon lifted him with the ease of a man carrying a child, she realized weight was hardly an issue.

He turned to look at her and said, "Where do you want him?"

Stone stepped up and said, "Before we take him to the fridge or cooler or call the local authorities, let's ask your cook if she knows him."

Kasha brightened. "Put him on one of the stretchers out here."

As they turned to the door, Merk had joined them with a gurney. They laid the man down on the surface and threw a sheet over him. Merk and Stone pushed the dead man to join Bullard in the war room. A quick conversation between Kasha and Tahlia and then a look at the dead man underneath the sheet had determined that the cook did not know the armed intruder.

Merk left Stone in the war room to relieve Harrison on the rooftop.

Brandon raised his eyebrows at Kasha's translation, turned and whispered to her, "That look of surprise on Tahlia's face could be at seeing her first dead man, though I doubt that with her village full of bad guys."

"You still think she's lying to us, don't you?"

Brandon nodded as he walked back into the room where he'd shot the man, and Kasha followed. "What are you looking for?"

"I want to know what he was doing in here. I want to know why he was here. I want to know what the hell he thought he was doing in the holding. And how the hell he got inside."

"You didn't buy the story from the others that they were looking for work?"

"Maybe. In a way, yes, especially if Bullard put out the call. Hundreds of them will be coming. The problem is, this guy was inside, and the only other person inside was your cook." He turned to look at Kasha. "And why didn't the heat sensors pick up his presence earlier?"

"It doesn't work on this floor," she admitted. "Bullard knew that, but we didn't have time to fix it."

"Well, that's not good."

BRANDON DIDN'T MEAN it to come out that way. But, being in a country like this—where betrayal and deceit seemed to be served at breakfast and lunch and dinner—it was a little hard to trust anyone. His heart had damn near come to a full stop when he'd heard the gunfire. It had been all he could do to force her to the floor and out of the way of the bullet. He'd felt a tug on his shoulder as it had passed him, but thankfully it hadn't done any damage.

"Why back here? How many floors are above us? Four? He was in here for a reason." Brandon stared at the crates stacked around this smaller room. "What's in this stuff?"

"No idea." She shrugged. "We didn't have time to open

up the crates and inventory this stuff before. We were planning to come back in a couple weeks. We stayed longer than planned as it was for our first visit. This was supposed to be a quick trip in and out, but …"

Brandon turned to study where the man had been hiding, finding a corner space hidden by boxes with a pallet on the floor, a canteen, beef jerky and nuts. He shook the canteen and heard nothing. "He's been here for a while. There's all kinds of computer equipment out in the open in this room."

"Computers were everywhere when we arrived. But older versions with no logical setup, just a jumbled mess. We shoved it all in here so we could set up our gear properly."

He turned to face her. "Do we know for sure the previous owner is gone?"

She frowned. "No. It's not as if I saw a death certificate. But, like I said, it was supposed to be empty for close to five years. But, when we saw all this stuff, we assumed a squatter had been here." She took a deep breath and added, "We did have trouble the first day we were here. We had a group of men come by and threaten Bullard. They wanted him to get the hell out of here."

Brandon stared at her. "And you're just mentioning this now?"

"I thought you knew already," she protested. "Besides, Bullard just laughed it off."

Brandon shook his head, pissed. "Did anyone tell Ice?"

She frowned "Bullard did. At least I think he did."

Brandon had to wonder. Maybe Bullard didn't tell Ice everything after all.

Chapter 4

KASHA CHECKED THE time. "Dave will be calling in soon. And I need to see how Bullard is."

Brandon nodded and followed her into the ER room off the main war room. After noting Bullard's vitals on a clipboard, she watched over her boss. He showed no signs of coming out of his drugged stupor. She wanted to get him home, but he'd been very specific about not changing the flight schedule. She hated that. That left the onus on her to follow his instructions, but, if things went bad, she didn't want something to happen to him because she couldn't decide for herself. Her phone rang as she sat at Bullard's side. She set it up for a video conference again. "Hey, Dave. Right on time."

"How is he?" Dave's total focus was on the unconscious man on the stretcher.

"No change so far, yet his vitals remain strong. Which is good, right?"

Dave nodded. "I would think so."

"Although we did find needle marks on the inside of his elbow, where he was injected with drugs. Nothing else would explain his state."

"The trouble is, we don't know what drugs were used or how much was given him or if it was just one drug or a cocktail. All those details matter."

"Right. And we haven't even gotten Bullard into a warm bath, as our search for medical supplies ended when we found an armed intruder, who Brandon killed in self-defense. And now we probably shouldn't move Bullard from the central war room to any bathtub in this place. Although his body is no longer as chilled."

Dave sighed. "I'm sending the plane early. The pilot will be there around 4:00 a.m."

Fourteen hours to go. She grinned. "Perfect."

"I see the five of you. Where are the others?"

"Merk and Harrison are surveying the area. Keeping watch."

"Do you think you're under attack?"

"Not yet, but we suspect it's coming."

"Why?"

"I'm not sure what's going on with the mercs in town, but remember the trouble we had before you and I left Bullard alone here? It's quite possible something is brewing locally. Maybe nobody wanted Bullard to have the place."

"Or maybe somebody was using the place and wants their base back," Brandon added. "The squatter's computer equipment, even if not up to our caliber, would be expensive to replace for a small faction far away from any cities and tech companies. Or they could want the information they have stored on it."

"Who knows what else is here that they left behind," Kasha said. "And we've had too many interruptions to inventory the place properly."

"As a stronghold, it's a nice setup," Dave said. "I can send a team of men if you need them."

"We should plan to leave a team here until Bullard is healthy and a full security system is properly installed here."

"Okay, I'll send four men on the plane." He smirked. "I know just who to send."

"That's a good idea. Send some rations for them too. It looks like the kitchen has been cleaned out."

"Of course it has." Dave's voice was resigned. "It seems like we're always up against renegades and thieves."

"We could've gone anywhere in the world, but this is where Bullard wanted to be."

"I think it was more a case of the rules were a whole lot less restricted there," Dave said drily.

"True enough." She hung up to find Brandon waiting for her, one eyebrow raised, and Stone nearby.

"Dave's sending the plane a little earlier, depending on the weather conditions. He doesn't like the drug's effect on Bullard."

Brandon checked Bullard's pulse. "The problem is, they could have given him a horse tranquilizer, and he'll be knocked out for days."

"Dave's also sending more men. They'll stay here to protect the property when we leave."

"That's a good idea, with evidence of a squatter, long before we had to kill that armed intruder. I think a rebel group was using the holding. When it was sold, they probably didn't know it until Bullard showed up. In which case, they probably want to retrieve their equipment." Brandon turned and stepped to the open doorway to look at all the computers in the war room. "Is this all Bullard's equipment?"

She nodded. "We set this up when we arrived. The squatter's equipment is in the side room where that guy surprised us."

He pivoted to face her and said, "In that case I want to

take a really good look at what they have in there."

With Tahlia and Stone standing watch beside Bullard, Kasha walked with Brandon to the nearby room. "We stored it all in here because we didn't know where else to put it or who it belonged to. Since we bought the property, everything legally belonged to us when we took over, but it was also supposed to be basically empty so ..."

He nodded and didn't say anything. She turned on the light and pointed out the boxes, crates, monitors and laptops.

He shook his head. "This could be something they'd be after. Or the data stored therein. They'll come back after this gear. What about the armory? Was it fully loaded too when Bullard bought the place, when he took possession of this property?"

She frowned. "Some of it was here. Bullard was crowing over the older guns."

Brandon nodded. "That's more likely what this is about. The trouble is, we don't know how many men are coming to reclaim their property." He went to a laptop, turned it on and then pulled out two more from the stack and turned them on. "Let's see what they're up to."

"Do you think we should?"

"We definitely should," he said quietly. "We don't know what kind of an illegal operation they were running here. But, if it's big news, it could also be extremely bad news."

She stood at his side as he searched through the laptops.

"None of these are password-protected. There's all kinds of data, and none of their search histories have been cleared. They probably had no idea they would lose control over their base of operation."

"Well, they should have. It wasn't theirs to keep." She

laughed. "They knew they didn't own this property."

"There are a lot of deserted buildings in this country, lending itself to the squatter's mentality."

"That doesn't make it theirs." She considered the massive amount of money tied up even in the older equipment here and realized he was probably right. Somebody was running an illegal operation from here. "What if that's what the mercenaries were actually doing? Maybe they were just using Bullard's call for hired help as a cover for their presence in town. Maybe they were in the area already because they've been living here. In Bullard's new holding."

"Anything's possible." But Brandon's voice had an absentminded tone to it.

She leaned over his shoulder to look at the Excel document he had up. "What is that?"

"Arms sales."

She took a step back and said, "What?"

He didn't even turn to look at her. "We need to see if the squatters are the ones selling the weapons and to who. Because, if they are, they'll not only come back but they'll come back in full force, and they'll blow this place to shit to take it over."

"They just want their stuff back though," she said quickly. "Right?"

"Sure. But they'll also want possession of the place again. I highly doubt too many places have this much potential to store huge caches of inventory and men, plus would work so perfectly for what their needs would entail, like a defensive post out in the middle of nowhere with little interference from locals or authorities. Which is exactly why Bullard wanted it. He's the one who bought and paid for it, so it's his. However, not only do we have to protect him but we have to get him back on his feet so he can find a way to make peace with whoever was living here. Or take them out."

He motioned toward the sealed boxes and crates on the sides of the room. "We need to open up some of those and look inside. Let's figure out exactly what is here."

She said, "We should also check the floor-to-ceiling locked cabinets in the garage. We never did open them, because, well, we just didn't have time."

He lifted his gaze and pinned her in place. "What locked cabinets?"

She gave him a small smile. "Come with me."

He stepped away from the laptops and said, "Let's go."

She moved quickly to the garage. On the left was a wall of cabinets. A new lock was on one of the large double doors. He examined it and pulled out some tool from his back pocket. Within seconds he had the lock open.

She shook her head. "You did that a little too quickly for my liking."

"We picked up all kinds of skills in the military," he said. He removed the lock and slowly propped open the large doors. They both stood and stared. Shelves and shelves of semiautomatic weapons.

"Oh, shit," she said, her hands on the top of her head. "I don't think Bullard knew about this."

Two other doors were padlocked, but the locks were older. Brandon opened them and found the entire wall was full of various weapons. "Well, the only good thing is, we won't be short on artillery. But it also means, whoever's missing all this equipment will do an awful lot to get it back."

Merk walked in, took one look and whistled. "What the hell is this?"

Brandon explained. "This is bigger trouble than we were expecting."

"Is this all of it?"

"No," Brandon snapped. "In the room where we ran into the shooter is all the computer equipment Bullard found when he took possession of the property. He stored it all together there. I found at least three laptops and an Excel document with arms sales before we got sidetracked into checking out these cabinets. But those laptops were out in the open in that storage room on the first floor. No telling what we'll find when we open up the sealed boxes and crates in that room." With a shake of his head, he added, "Plus I took three keys off the armed intruder. Gave them to Stone. They might be the keys to the three padlocks I just picked to find all these weapons."

"Harrison and I came down for a short break and sent Stone alone up on the rooftop for now. But we need two men up there at all times. Stone can check into the key situation on his next break, but I'm pretty sure the armed intruder's keys will fit each of these locks."

"So we've got trouble." Kasha asked, "The question is, what are we supposed to do about it?"

Merk shook his head. "Let's lock these up again, make sure the garage is secured, so it's harder for intruders to get in. Then let's finish checking out that room with the squatter's laptops."

They locked up everything, glanced around to see if anything else was hidden here and walked out, locking the interior door behind them.

Back in the computer storage room, Brandon showed Merk the laptops and the Excel document. Harrison awaited them in the war room but moved to stand equidistant between Bullard and the storage room so Harrison could hear their discussion.

Once Merk realized Brandon was correct, Merk said, "Let's see exactly what's going on here." They went through the boxes and moved them off several wooden crates underneath. "Were these here originally?" he asked Kasha.

"It is one of the reasons Bullard wanted to put the rest of the stuff in here. He figured it was all left behind by the same people. He was trying to keep it all separate from his stuff."

A crowbar was off to the side. Merk picked it up and popped open the lid of a crate to find it full of hand grenades. He squatted and studied the markings on the case. "This is military grade." He turned to look at Brandon. "This isn't just an arms deal. This is somebody loading for war."

Kasha shook her head. "It looks like a lot. But it's not a lot for a full-fledged war."

"Maybe not," Merk said. "But what about all those?"

She spun around to see the crates lining the back wall from floor to ceiling. She hadn't considered what might be inside them. If they were full of grenades, more weapons … She could feel the color draining from her face. "Who do we call?"

"Levi," Merk said. "We need to know what to do with all this."

"We keep it, for now," Brandon replied. "Like Bullard would say, the sale was as is. Everything on the grounds is his. The trouble is, we have to make sure the people who bought all these toys aren't coming back, expecting to do a late pickup."

"You know they're on their way," Merk said. "We've already had proof of that in the village. The question is, are those mercenaries part of the team coming in, or were they serious about looking for work and might be on our side?" Merk shook his head, already dialing his phone. "I'll relieve Harrison, send him up to help Stone." He stepped out of the room.

Brandon could hear Merk's voice in the background. He stood and stared at the crates. "This is huge. A lot of money is tied up in this equipment."

"Nobody'll let this kind of money go. I can't imagine what they were trying to do with all this except sell it," Kasha said.

"Or use it themselves and overthrow the government," Brandon offered. "That seems to be a common theme in countries over here. Alternatively, selling it would bring in a lot of cash. On the open market, the stuff's worth millions."

"Right, so do we call the military and have these collected, or do we contact the villagers and provide them a way to protect themselves from the mercs, or do we keep it?" Kasha asked.

"For the most part, what we have to do is protect it," Brandon said. "What we don't want is to let all this firepower get into the hands of a rebel group."

"I can't say I really want the local government to have it either," Kasha said. "They haven't been in power longer than half a minute. There are more coups and ousted governments around this area than anything else. Of course, it's not just in Benin. It's everywhere. Large and small countries are being overthrown on a regular basis."

Brandon shrugged. "It's the same in many parts of the world." He opened several cardboard boxes to find monitors. "Did you pack these up?"

She shook her head. "Bullard and a couple guys and I

would have looked into all the unsealed boxes just to confirm it wasn't Bullard's equipment before moving it all here. But we didn't fully unpack the boxes to inspect everything that could be in each one. After all, if we found an old wired mouse and its 8"x10" mouse pad on top of the box, we knew this was someone else's used computer parts, not something Bullard brought with him. So I just put stuff back into the boxes we had pulled from them."

"That makes sense. And you had no idea who was here before you took possession of the property?"

She shook her head. "No. There was no one here to hand over possession. We were given the keys through the property brokers."

"And that didn't raise any alarms?"

She frowned. "Of course it did. Bullard contacted the agent, and he said he was here six months ago, and it was completely empty. Since whoever was here was squatting, they forfeited all their rights."

Brandon looked at her and said, "We should ask Tahlia a few more questions than we have so far."

"Do you really think she has anything to do with this?"

"I'm damn sure she knows a whole lot more than she's letting on."

BRANDON CONSIDERED HOW many toys he'd brought with him for this job. They were the latest and best versus the equipment he'd found here in this computer storage room. Although a lot of equipment was gathered here, it looked old and outdated to him. And would have looked really old to Bullard as well. All he'd cared about was getting set up. He could imagine Bullard setting up his latest and greatest command center, like a boy with a brand-new toy. Honestly, if this was his place, Brandon would be over the moon. It was an incredible stronghold. But one still had to brush out all the spiders before one set up shop.

And, in this case, the spiders had fangs, as Bullard had found out. He should've come in with a full-on team and swept the area, cleaned it all out and made sure the neighborhood was fully aware of who was now in power at the stronghold. This was Africa. And the more undeveloped part.

Brandon knew, once Bullard was back on his feet, that issue would be taken care of in no time. If there was one thing Bullard knew how to do, it was handling opposition and making friends as needed in nearby villages. But, until then, Brandon and the guys had to make sure Bullard was okay. Brandon himself was all about stepping forward with guns in hand to protect Bullard's property, but that wasn't necessarily the best way forward long-term.

Brandon didn't have a ton of political skill; he was much more a knock-'em-down, settle-it-with-a-fistfight type of a guy. He had very little patience for thieves and squatters and mercs and kidnappers. He understood needing a place to sleep against the cold. But the mercs had attempted to turn this property into an arms dealership, funding a civil war maybe. That would not go down well with Bullard, once he woke up.

Until then Brandon was on the spot right now, and that meant he'd do what he could to protect Bullard and his people and his property—even using the stockpile of guns and ammo here, no matter how old. He turned to look at Bullard, hating to see the big man down. Bullard was a man in his prime, used to being in a position of power and control. Everything Brandon had heard and read about Bullard said he would use power with a soft but stern hand.

That Brandon could admire. But, in the meantime, he was more than a little worried about the oncoming night. He sat down at the laptop, glanced at the time—4:10 p.m.—and then at Kasha. "I suggest you talk to Tahlia while there are no men around. See if you can get any information out of her."

Kasha nodded and stepped out. He watched her leave. Her loyalty was something he could also admire. At the same time, he hoped it wasn't misplaced. He didn't want her to be susceptible to people like Tahlia. He hoped the older cook was exactly what she appeared to be.

He had seen some twisted things in his life. The one thing he knew about all those rebel soldiers out there, they all had moms. As soon as that family relationship popped up, those moms defended, lied, cheated and stole for their sons.

He shook his head, returned his attention to one of the laptops, bringing up an internet browser and checking the history.

It made for fascinating reading. Government rules, laws, regulations, locations and GPS coordinates. It looked like the discussion was all about a sale and its delivery. Brandon wondered if maybe somebody should be out there intercepting that proposed sale. If the money had already been paid, then a lot of people would be pissed off if the delivery wasn't completed.

That was another reason the upcoming night would be a little more dangerous than usual. They didn't want anybody to make it in as far as this location. Bullard was still unconscious. That made him an easy target. They had to look after three people, if they counted Kasha. And, in his mind, he counted Kasha. She'd be mad if she knew what he was thinking right now. She was strapped with two pistols, but she was still female. He knew it was archaic, but his mentality said he still needed to keep an eye out for the women and children.

She was all woman—lean, curvy and intelligent. There was nothing to not like. As a package, she had a slightly exotic air to her with that dark hair complemented by her fairer skin. Her voice had a wonderful accent. He didn't know how many languages she spoke, but he suspected several. The Arabic just flew off her lips in an easy tumble of the language. He didn't understand a word she said to the cook. He hated that. He sat back and thought about how his mind worked. His years in the military hadn't given him a rosy-hued view of life.

He'd spent way too much time dealing with governments, either falling down or being propped up, only to fall again under another coup a few weeks later. Then there were his tours in Afghanistan. Eye-opening experiences. He'd traveled most of the world. But it wasn't like he got to travel in the daylight.

Everything was undercover, in the dark of night. He'd been air-dropped out of planes many times for clandestine landings. He had yet to go to most of the countries as a tourist. He saw shaky governments and poor economic scenarios—armies more on the take than not. Most people saw the acres of plantations and tourist attractions and the beautiful blue waters surrounding the countries.

He hadn't been blessed with that viewpoint.

He checked a couple email programs just in case whoever had been using the laptop had left himself logged in. Sure enough, as Brandon clicked around, a screen opened to show an inbox. He checked the name, didn't recognize it, but took a picture with his phone. Then he scanned the emails. Just in case he lost possession of the machine, he took photographs of every one. He was right in thinking this was an arms-dealing operation.

There were multiple discussions on prices, orders, shipments and supplies. Delivery arrangements had been made for the following morning.

Yet the gunrunners couldn't make the delivery as Bullard's team had been here the past week and now Levi's team was sitting on the arms. Looking through the emails, Brandon confirmed the gunrunners had already been paid. That just added to the pressure. They'd *have* to come after the weapons soon.

He hopped to his feet, grabbed the laptop and raced out to the others. Merk was just getting off the phone. He looked up and said, "I've updated Levi, Ice and Dave. Then Levi and Ice got their heads together, made some calls. It's been a phonefest out here. What did you find?"

"Proof of an arms deal Monday morning. *Tomorrow.* We have bank accounts. We have names. We have locations." He flipped the laptop around to show the open inbox.

Merk's eyebrows rose. "Oh, shit. We need to send this to Ice."

"And Dave," Kasha said. "He can make a decision about what we'll do. This is Bullard's property."

"Between them and Kasha," Brandon said, "they can reach a mutual decision on Bullard's behalf. But, in the meantime, we need to defend this place, and we'll be outnumbered for sure." Brandon shook his head. "The gunrunners have been paid. They need to get the weapons in order to make that delivery tomorrow. That means they'll be here tonight."

From that moment on there was nothing but organized chaos. Phone calls, emails, images being sent back and forth. The big wall screen in the war room was opened to the GPS location of Bullard's newest holding and the surrounding area. Brandon looked at Merk and said, "I'll get Harrison and Stone. We need them in on this."

Merk nodded. "You do that. And fast. We don't have much time. It'll be dark soon. They'll come then."

"I know. We could sure use those four additional men Dave is sending us right now. Not later when our flight comes in."

With a hard look between them, Brandon headed off to find Harrison and Stone. He found Stone first on the rooftop walkway.

Stone took one look at Brandon's face and asked, "What's up?"

"Lots. Also a change of plans. The flight's coming earlier with four additional men but probably not soon enough. We are caught up in the middle of some prepaid weapons deal going down first thing tomorrow. I have a suspicion we'll be under attack very soon."

Stone said, "Go bring Harrison up to speed and take him down below. I'll be fine here."

Brandon found Harrison standing watch on the opposite side of the roof and explained the situation. Still talking, they walked downstairs to the big central war room.

"Keeping the owner drugged as a captive to pull off an arms' deal out of his newly purchased property," Harrison said quietly, "we've certainly seen worse atrocities." They passed the entrance to the war room to head to the ER where everybody was gathered to be closer to Bullard.

They looked down at Bullard, covered with blankets, still unconscious on a stretcher. Brandon reached out a hand, checking his pulse. It was slow and steady.

"I hate to see him like this," Merk said.

"Have you known him long?" Brandon asked.

"On and off for years. He's a good man. He runs a team equivalent to Levi's. The fact that this happened to him just makes me angry."

Harrison said, "He was looking at an empty property, not expecting to get caught up in a civil war event with arms dealers."

The others nodded.

"Doesn't change the fact that's exactly what happened," Merk added.

Brandon turned to head toward Kasha who was clicking away on a keyboard. He looked at the monitor above her and asked, "Is that the location of the weapons deal?"

"I also found a couple other locations in the emails. I'm mapping them out to see exactly what we're looking at."

"Anybody hear back from Levi yet?" Brandon asked the group.

Merk nodded. "He's on it. So is Dave. They've decided to contact the local government, hard to do on a Sunday evening. Apparently the one currently in power is decent. They're looking for, and have been trying to flush out, several rebel groups hiding in the area. They think this might be one of them."

"Are the local authorities sending reinforcements?" Brandon asked. "I hope we won't need them, particularly when we're as well armed as we are. But the gunrunners might be happy to bring down the entire building on top of us rather than get caught."

"That won't allow them to retrieve the goods though." Merk smiled. "We have a military unit en route coming via land, so, in this isolated terrain, I don't expect them for another three hours at the soonest—hopefully a little after 9:00 p.m. Our return plane with four additional men is coming in an hour earlier if the pilot can swing it, but that still puts him getting here about 3:00 a.m. I suspect that'll be too late to help us. Bullard will be sorry he missed all the fun too."

"So will Levi, I imagine," Brandon said. "Seems like everybody wants a piece of the action."

"So very true," Kasha said. "I've never seen men more willing to go to war than Bullard and his group."

"Has this ever happened before?"

"Yes. I've been with him for five years. I've seen a lot during that time. We thought this would be a perfect location."

"If you think about it, it still is. Nothing has changed that. It's still very much Bullard style." Brandon turned to look at Kasha. "Were you planning to move here?"

She shook her head. "No. I'm returning to the US. I promised my family. My mom ..." She shrugged. "Not just that but it's time ..."

"It'd be hard to find another job like Bullard's."

"I know, right? He pays extremely well. I've really appreciated it. But maybe in a way he paid too well," she said on a laugh. "I can actually afford to go home now."

"You can always ask Levi for a job. I know they're talking about opening up a California office."

She looked up, interest in her eyes. "I've thought about it. Ice and I have talked about it even. Although I'm not sure

I'd want to stay in the same field."

"You could do something that had nothing to do with all this murder and mayhem," Brandon said. "It's not for everyone."

"My idea of total bliss is to have ten acres for myself somewhere," she said with a big smile. "It seems like, no matter where I turn, there are too many people around. And not always the good guys."

Brandon nodded. "Many of us have that same need for space and isolation. That's why Bullard builds his big holdings. They're his. He can keep everybody outside the gate. The only ones allowed in are the ones he lets in."

Just then Bullard released a heavy sigh.

Kasha leaned down and said, "Bullard, can you hear me?"

And damn if the big man didn't open his eyes.

Chapter 5

KASHA GENTLY PATTED Bullard's cheek. "Hey, boss. How are you feeling?"

Sluggish, his eyes unfocused, he rolled his head toward her voice.

She could see his eyelids moving, his eyes working to see her. "It's me, Kasha. We're still in the Benin stronghold. Don't force yourself to fully wake up. You were drugged." She could sense, more than see, the shock on his face.

He struggled to sit up, but the men forced him back down again. He glared at everyone, obviously still confused and disoriented.

Merk leaned over so it was his face Bullard saw. "It's Merk. We're here. We've got your back."

Bullard blinked several times and then said, "Merk?"

"Yeah. Just think, the day came when Bullard needed backup," Merk joked, but his hand on the big man's shoulder was gentle.

Bullard frowned as if trying to reorganize his thoughts.

Kasha watched as he tried to shrug and then shake his head, but his body wasn't working the way it was supposed to, and the movements came off jerky and uncoordinated.

"What happened?"

Kasha picked up the story and gave her boss a brief description of what they knew or had figured out. "But when I tell you that things are about to go to hell, you need to believe me," she said quietly. "We found a huge cache of weapons here. Cases and crates of machine guns, grenades, ammo."

His gaze narrowed as he struggled to comprehend the enormity of it. "Whose?" he tried to bark as usual, but it came out more of a puppy snarl.

She kept her smile hidden as she answered. "That we don't know yet. But we have their laptops. Remember when we arrived, how there was all the computer equipment, so much that we stacked it in a back room?"

He turned to look at her again, and she saw the comprehension in his eyes.

She added, "From that, we've discerned different locations, sales and even banking info. We're in their email system and what looks like a sales tracking document."

Merk added, "We have a lot of the names of people involved. But we're not sure of the hierarchy of who's selling, who's buying, who's the boss, who's screwing the government and which government they're trying to support."

As Bullard slowly understood, he groaned. "Just my luck. ... I figured this place was too good to be true." He reached up a shaky hand and rubbed his forehead. "I've been looking for a second holding, as Kasha can tell you." He slowly pointed a finger at her. "I was never sure of the wisdom of having just one place."

He coughed or laughed, Kasha wasn't sure.

"If I needed to go to ground, and my place was compromised, which has happened to me unfortunately a little too often, then I needed another location."

"Why so far away?" Merk asked.

"It seemed like the best idea." He cleared his throat. "I

could still get here by plane if I had to. I could drive if I had to. I could also fly by helicopter if I had to." He nodded in Merk's direction. "Sure, a place only a couple hours away by car would have been nice. But I couldn't find anything appropriate. As you guys know, it's all about layout, layout, layout."

"No, it's about location, location, location," Brandon said. "And this location sucks. We fetched you out of the village, and it's filled with mercs. Apparently you also put out the call you were looking for men. Is that correct?"

Bullard frowned. "I did say to somebody I was looking to hire staff—to run the holding, not for my teams. But that doesn't mean I want mercenaries for either position. As you know, we need the right men for this kind of company."

"The villagers down there were potentially telling the truth. They said they showed up because they heard you were looking to hire. Some of them were looking pretty ragged around the edges. Doesn't mean they're not good men though," Merk said.

"Just don't hire those six who held you captive in the village. I got their photos, and now Kasha has them downloaded too."

"Help me up," Bullard said and coughed. "It would be my luck to have them coming my way when I'm down."

Merk helped him sit up. "Some mercs may be decent, but some are scum. It's hard to know the difference unless you've known them a while or can trust who might have referred them. It takes time to trust someone you don't know, and putting them on a mission without that trust is hard. Unfortunately lots of mercenaries out there—on both sides—know who you are."

"Which is exactly why I never would have put out a call

like that. Too many people do know my name." He gasped, then coughed several times. "That means I could have been targeted right from the beginning."

"You might have. But it's also possible these men came for many other reasons."

Kasha walked back to the computer. "Don't forget they could also be the arms dealers themselves, trying to figure out how to get back into the holding. Making plans even as we stand here, holding Bullard up."

"Well, considering Brandon killed the one here," Harrison said with a laugh, "when their man never returned, it's guaranteed they'll come back with lots of firepower."

Bullard exchanged a grim look with each of them. "Sounds like we have work to do."

Brandon said, "Sorting out firepower first. We've got their grenades. But that doesn't mean they don't have rocket launchers. Just because the gunrunners left lots of weaponry here, we don't know what they removed before you arrived."

That startled a gasp from Kasha. "Are you serious?"

Harrison nodded. "Yes, absolutely he's serious. What you need to count on is that, no matter what's here, they've got equal, if not way worse, weaponry on their side. We just have to make sure we take them out first."

WITH BULLARD FEELING better, plans had to be made and put into action quickly. Tahlia set about making meals while Kasha ran coordination from the war room. Bullard had been rolled in there so he was nearby too. It was her job to stop Bullard from doing too much. She gave everybody a hard look when she heard that tacked-on duty. "You know nobody's going to stop Bullard, right?"

The others just grinned and nodded.

She sighed. "But I'll do my best."

Bullard snickered. "Lucky for you I don't feel like I can do very much now."

Brandon and Harrison headed to the weapons in the garage. They needed to make sure they had enough weaponry already loaded and sorted out for each man here. Plus Kasha. They also needed to know if they could use anything else in the computer storage room. Those grenades for one thing, but the last thing they wanted to do was damage Bullard's secondary headquarters. After ninety minutes of inventorying the cache, Brandon got the call to come eat. Since it was 7:40 p.m., he had to admit he was famished.

He looked over at Harrison, and they high-fived each other and returned to the war room. Tahlia had brought trays of food to them, serving plates of rice and beans, covered in a meat curry. Brandon didn't know what the meat was, but he was so hungry that it didn't matter.

While he ate heartily, he listened. These people were pros. He could still learn a lot from them. Being part of the military was often just a case of following orders, even if you disagreed. Brandon was rarely allowed any input into the military's tactical arrangements. Here it was different. Everyone had a say. Everybody discussed plans and strategies.

"The plane is now arriving even earlier with reinforcements. We hope it's here before 10:00 p.m.," Kasha said. "Bullard just received confirmation."

Brandon studied Bullard now sitting up and drinking a cup of coffee. "Are you sure coffee is good for you in your state?" he asked in a half-teasing voice.

Bullard grinned. There was something fierce in the look in his eye. "Try to take my coffee away from me, and you'll see just how alert I am."

Brandon grinned. "I've heard lots about you, something about a grizzly bear under attack."

Bullard chuckled. "That might be true. Right now I need the coffee, and then I'll try some of that food. Tahlia is a great cook."

Brandon studied the older woman, who even now was trying to stay in the background. She looked nervous. But then she probably understood they were getting a ton of weapons ready for an attack. He glanced around to see who was missing. "Has Merk gone to watch?"

Stone walked in just then. He nodded to Brandon. "You're up next."

Brandon finished his food and grabbed a cup of coffee. "I'll go out now." As he left, he noticed Harrison behind him. He raised an eyebrow. "Are you coming too?"

"Yes, there'll be two of us every time. Trying to keep watch on the entire place takes more eyes than we have right now. But we definitely don't want a lone lookout person taken down to leave the rest of us vulnerable."

Upstairs they relieved Merk. He was happy to see them coming. "I can smell dinner from here," he said with a big smile. "I really hope you didn't eat it all."

Harrison grinned and smacked Merk on the shoulder. "No, lots of food for you. Go on down now. The two of us will be here for the next two hours."

"Are we doing two-hour rotations?" Brandon asked, Merk still hanging around for this discussion.

Harrison nodded. "We're expecting them any time. We've loaded the machine guns, so one for each of us is getting readied with extra ammo. Bullard is taking down the serial numbers for each gun and even keeping track of the ammo."

"Why? Is he charging us for them?" Merk asked jokingly.

Brandon chuckled. "No, he's likely expecting grief from the military whenever they arrive."

Harrison opened his vest. It was lined with grenades. He also had two handguns. Merk took one look and whistled. "But no machine guns."

"Bullard's clearing them right now. We should have them in thirty minutes."

Merk nodded and headed downstairs, calling back, "I'll bring you the weapons when he's done."

On the rooftop walkway, Brandon and Harrison walked together. After they had done one full round, they split up and each headed in different directions, so they would meet on the other side. Moving slowly, Brandon studied the hillsides. Darkness was settling in. It threw long shadows on the surrounding areas. He wished he'd had enough time to get used to the geographical landmarks before night fell. All they could do now was watch for movement and reflections and listen for noises that shouldn't be there. He moved soundlessly in the night, sticking close to the wall but watchful of the gun ports. The last thing he wanted was to get picked off by a sharpshooter.

On the other side, the two nodded and continued around. They kept up their slow, steady movement for five rounds and then ducked down and waited. Harrison raised an eyebrow. "Now they should be wondering where we've gone to."

"No, they'll expect us to have left. We did our rounds but got lazy because there's no action."

Harrison nodded. "Let's go look at the rifle slots in the

wall, count them, see how far apart they are."

Brandon saw one he'd noticed earlier. "We should text Merk and see what the holdup is on the weapons." He ducked, using his body and his free hand to shield the light from his phone as he checked it briefly to see the time. It was after 8:00 p.m.

Harrison already had his cell phone out and was heading to the stairwell to hide before texting Merk.

Within minutes, they heard a hawk's call. Harrison responded in kind. Moving silently in the night, Merk arrived and gave each of them one of the semiautomatic machine guns, along with an ammo belt. In a low voice, he said, "Locked and loaded."

Then he took up a position on the opposite side. Now three were on rooftop watch.

That meant only Stone was downstairs with Bullard, Tahlia and Kasha. Brandon knew he didn't have any proof for the way he was feeling, but he didn't trust Tahlia. It could be because he didn't understand her language and the fact she was here when they arrived, along with that armed intruder in the computer storage room. That could mean all kinds of things. But what it didn't do was raise any sense of security about her. His instincts weren't firing up red flags but neither were they comfortable with her in the building.

The three men continued to roam the rooftop walkway silently, making sure nobody had anything shiny. A sharpshooter didn't have to see your form. He just had to aim at the reflection and shoot. At one point, Brandon squatted flat against the chest-high stone wall to look out a gun port. And froze. *What was that?*

As Harrison crept up beside him, Brandon held out his hand with one finger up. He watched silently. Instead of looking directly at the area where there was movement, he turned his head slightly to the side and let the movement be caught by his peripheral vision. And there it was. He saw a second one. He raised a second finger for Harrison. Harrison rose up slowly beside him. He waited and watched too. In a low tone he said, "I only see two."

"Two *here*."

With the enemy's position marked, Harrison ducked low and raced around to Merk. If the intruders were smart, they would have the entire place surrounded. They had put enough men in the little village to do a full-on assault. But, if they did that, they wouldn't have any men leftover for a second run. Too often people put all their best men out front, hoping to take it in one go, but, once they lost half their men, they were not able to finish. Better to be stealthy and strategic. Loss of life in a situation like this was critical.

Brandon kept watch, but the two men out on the hillside before him never moved. That meant they were waiting, which could mean the main attack was coming from another area.

He turned from the east side wall and slunk along the wall until he was in position between Merk and Harrison, with the north, west and south sides covered by them respectively. He studied the plateau around the holding. It took him a good ten minutes for his eyes to adjust to the receding light. But once they did, he picked up four men creeping along the ground. He again shielded his phone screen as he sent a short text to Kasha in the command center that they had two invading men on the east and four bogeys on the west. Within seconds, he had Harrison at his side. He whispered, "Merk has two on his side too."

"Full frontal here then," Brandon said. "What about the

fourth side?"

Merk whispered, "I'll check it out. Back in five." He disappeared, his footsteps soundless on the stone. The four men approaching slowed and came to a stop. They were about one hundred yards off. Brandon could certainly pick them off, but he wanted to see what they were going to do first.

He was surrounded and outnumbered. Quite possibly also outgunned—depending on what the enemy had with them.

But Brandon also had several advantages they didn't. He was higher up, and it was much easier to shoot downward. He had more-than-enough ammo to wipe out every person in the village ten times over. He was behind a wall and protected. Those men were out in the open, hoping stealth would get them inside the security wall. That was the priority for Brandon and the others: to make sure nobody breached the perimeter wall.

Harrison was back in minutes. "There are two more. We need another person up on this rooftop." He disappeared again.

Keeping an eye on the four men, with his machine gun ready to fire, Brandon was surprised to hear Kasha's voice come up beside him. He stiffened and turned to look at her. She had the same weaponry as he did, and she was crouched beside him, hiding below the wall, but with the machine gun just barely resting on top where there was a crack in the stone. It was a very good position.

She stared at him, a knowing smirk on her face. "Just because I'm female doesn't mean I don't know what I'm doing."

He grinned but tried not to show his white teeth.

"Sweetheart, you can play war games with me any time."

She gave a quiet half laugh.

Outside, still nobody made a move.

Brandon had to wonder what they were waiting for.

Chapter 6

KASHA STUDIED THE man crouched beside her. His long lean body had relaxed in a deceptively casual position. He had that panther type of movement, which showed perfect awareness and control. He didn't have to stomp or storm to show he was bigger and stronger than everybody else—he just looked it. But he was so in control that there was a gracefulness to him. It was part of his DNA.

She had to appreciate that. Power was dead sexy, and speaking of dead, she turned to peer through her gun port to see where the attackers came from. She could see all four lying flat in the sand, almost camouflaged in their brown khakis. But once she knew where they were, it was easy to see them. "What do you think they're waiting for?"

"That's what I'm trying to figure out," Brandon said calmly. "Usually a diversion. For a signal to start. It could also be they're waiting for more company."

She gazed at him, startled. "How do you figure?"

"There are two options, the way I see it. They could be waiting for their own reinforcements, or they are waiting for ours to arrive to attack them. If Dave's men fly in, they will be in the line of fire but don't forget that they'll be packing a lot of firepower themselves. If the four new guys are attacked by a machine gun mounted on a truck, we'd have to take out the driver first and foremost, and, if anybody's operating a gun in an open truck bed, then he's got to go next."

She nodded, understanding. "I know what to do," she said. "I just don't have the same level of experience you do."

"I wish you didn't have to have any," Brandon admitted. "I'd like to believe in a world where there was no war and women and children were safe. But we don't live in that world. So chances are good that, before this night's out, you will have plenty of practice."

"Levi keeps sending transmissions. Seems Dave's idea to send more men meant more of Levi's men. So Levi's sending more men."

Brandon grinned. "Sounds like he doesn't trust us."

"You think you should be able to handle all this?"

"Absolutely. But there's no doubt Bullard will need more help to keep his power in place at this holding. He must recover from this attack and create a decent relationship with the entire village. So it'll take more than four men."

"The plane might be delayed. Apparently they needed to pick up someone at another location."

Brandon shrugged. "We're not helpless. We have water. We have food. We have weapons. Better than that, we're protected. Whatever these assholes want to do, they can bring it on."

She found herself settling at his confidence. He wasn't cocky. He wasn't arrogant. He was just sure of himself. Knowledgeable in the ways of war that she hoped she'd never become. Shooting was hard—and it should be hard. But, in a situation where it was down to her or them, she was all for having a gun and using it.

She'd tried to talk to Tahlia again to see what was going on, but Tahlia hadn't been forthcoming. She lived in the village and had a family. She'd been hoping to be hired by Bullard, and, when he had arrived, he had hired her. But she found it hard working at the holding. Going back and forth to the village was tough. Everybody in the village kept questioning her. Still, Kasha couldn't help wondering if Tahlia was either hiding more or she really was oblivious to what was going on around her. Kasha had a lot of trouble with that concept.

"Tahlia has two sons," she offered.

Brandon studied her face. "Any chance they're out here?"

"I don't know." She turned a worried look his way. "But she's the only one down there with Bullard."

He pulled out his phone and handed it to Kasha. "Tell Bullard to watch out for her. There's nothing like having a viper in the nest."

Troubled, she hesitated.

"Warn him," Brandon urged. "At least then he's on guard. What we don't want is for her to turn around and put a bullet in him while we're all up here. If she even shows herself on this roof, I'll take her out," he promised.

Kasha frowned. "She could just be scared and looking for help. Maybe she'll run upstairs to us."

"Maybe she'll run upstairs with a gun of her own."

That shut her up. She did as Brandon warned and shielded the phone screen to send a text to Bullard, telling him to keep a gun close—not to trust Tahlia. Bullard's response came back immediately.

She smiled. As she handed the phone back, she said, "Bullard says he's watching her."

Brandon nodded. "Bullard seems like a good guy."

"He is."

"So how come you want to leave him?"

She shook her head. "It's not that I want to leave him. But a part of me would like to leave the lifestyle. Do something else. But it's so ingrained in me now, I'm not sure I can," she admitted. "Maybe a job with less danger?"

Brandon studied her features in the half-light. "Less shooting, killing, the necessity of it all?"

"Yeah. I'd like to have a small place of my own. Maybe even a garden and a few animals."

"What would you like to do for work?"

"I'll find something," she promised. "I'm just not sure I want to keep doing *this*."

"You're pretty young for a midlife crisis."

"I'm thirty."

Clearly startled, he flashed that white grin at her, then remembered to shield it too. "You don't look like you're over twenty-four."

Inside she smiled. "Don't get distracted," she chuckled, "by my good looks."

He gave her a horrified look and peered over the top again. "They're still there and haven't moved." His phone vibrated. He pulled it out and checked a text. "Merk's got movement."

She got to her feet. "I'm heading his way. Be back in a few minutes." She moved quietly down the rooftop walkway toward Merk. Once at his side she asked, "What have you got?"

"Two more have arrived."

"So there's twelve now?" She had to admit that she didn't like the odds.

Merk smiled. "Now we're starting to have some fun. I would expect more coming on Stone's side."

"We're already outmanned," she said, worried. "We don't want them to have more men."

"We are not only outnumbered but probably outgunned too. Yet it won't make a damn bit of difference. We can pick them all off from here."

She studied his face and smiled. "I guess that's why Bullard calls you guys when he needs help, huh?"

"Absolutely. We're all the same flock. You know, if Bullard was up here, he'd already have started the charge."

She had to admit that, whenever there was a problem, Bullard was the one who jumped in first. He figured, if he stopped the fight before it really got started, he could get a good shit-kicking in, and nobody else would get one on him. Something he really enjoyed. She never quite understood, but it seemed to be very much a macho male thing. Maybe it was part of why she was looking to leave. She didn't know exactly; she just wanted something different. She'd been around so many military operations and was saddened at the need for them. At the same time, she wanted something else for her life. She said, "I'll go check on Stone."

She turned and crept along the rooftop, got all the way back around the complex to where Stone was the only one standing. The two of them were evenly spaced around the walkway. The stone wall rose on the outside chest high so they could still look over the rampart. As she approached Stone, she said, "How many men do you have out there?"

"Two and two more arriving, plus a text confirming another pair headed toward the east side."

"So we've got four at each station." She shook her head. "Not sure I like that."

Stone just smiled at her and said, "You should check on Tahlia and Bullard."

"I don't want to leave you guys alone up here."

"We'll be fine. For us, this is child's play. You get down there. Make sure she's not kicking Bullard's ass."

There was no humor in his tone, and she realized he was echoing her own worries. She went downstairs, and, as she headed toward the main war room, she stopped, her instincts kicking her back to flatten against the wall. Something was wrong, but she didn't know what.

"So you aren't really a cook. I wondered."

"Of course I'm cook," Tahlia snapped in broken English.

Kasha frowned, pissed. So Tahlia had been lying.

"You need to put that gun down," Bullard said in a quiet tone.

"Why would I? It's just the two of us. I have what the men want. I figured this would be my chance."

"Are you the one who drugged me?"

"Yes. I am. But they took you away from here pretty fast."

"So you put it in my food?"

"Yes, but it didn't take effect right away," she said in frustration. "You are too big. I didn't put enough in."

Kasha peered around the corner as Bullard extended his arms to show the needle tracks. "Yet they gave me more drugs when I was in the village."

"We had to. You kept fighting."

"Of course. This is my place now."

"If you were dead," she said flatly, "it would be ours again."

"My company still owns it. My men would still come look after it, clean it out to rid the vermin from here."

"It was our place," Tahlia snapped. "It is ours."

"It was *never* your place. You stole it. But I'm sure the finer nuances of the law don't bother you much considering you've already been drugging and killing people."

Kasha watched his gaze casually wander the room, catching sight of her and glossing over that event without even stopping. He turned his attention back to Tahlia and said, "It's too bad you're not really the cook. The food was pretty good tonight."

"Of course I'm a cook. I raised my sons. Every woman here cooks."

"Do all women here carry arms?"

She shook her head. "But we've had to. Times have been tough. So many of our men killed. We have no choice."

"Too bad," Bullard said. "Because I could have used you."

In front of Kasha's shocked gaze, he raised a handgun and shot Tahlia.

WITH HIS EYES adjusted to the light of the night, Brandon could see the men still lying in wait outside. He'd been waiting for Kasha to come back from checking on Merk, but there'd been no sign of her.

He lined up his sight to see the men, heads together in a heavy discussion. They were staying just out of range for pistols but not for machine guns or grenades. Regardless, any plans they were making wouldn't be good for him or the rest of his team. His cell phone vibrated. He shielded it as he pulled it out and checked the message from Merk. **I have four. They've moved ahead ten feet.**

Ten feet here too, Brandon answered. He waited for Stone to check in. Almost instantly Stone's report came back with a similar text. Brandon didn't want to ask about Kasha because he didn't want to appear to be worried about her. But when there was no response from her, he sent her a text and asked, **Is all okay?**

Her response came back fast. **Yes. No.**

What happened?

Be there in a few minutes.

He waited, but there was no sign of her. At the same time, his instincts were already rubbed raw, firing up all kinds of ideas of what had gone on. Was she still with Merk? Or had she gone downstairs? He kept an eye on the attackers creeping ever closer. Brandon had no intention of being pinned inside the unit. He could take out all four in ten seconds but wanted to see what they were up to. So what were they waiting for?

Then he heard a sound in the far distance, like a plane. He couldn't see it from here, but he could track the noise of it.

If it carried the four additional men Dave was sending, good. Except the invading men on the ground could easily have more men waiting for the plane to land and then to ambush them.

As the plane noise slowed and geared down, he watched to see what the attackers would do. They didn't move. Brandon counted on Levi's men taking them out in no time.

Just as he was ready to send another text to find out what happened to Kasha, he heard gunfire coming from where the airstrip was out of his sight. Grim, he waited with the four men down below in his crosshairs. He watched their expressions, but they didn't even turn around to look at the battle site.

In other words, they were expecting the plane. But was

that because they had a party waiting and expecting to take out the new arrivals easily? Then come down here and give them backup in attacking this holding?

If so, well, Brandon would count on Levi's team any day. But they had no idea what they'd be up against. Brandon heard footsteps coming up behind him. He stilled but then recognized the scent. "What's up, Kasha?"

"Levi's team has landed."

"Good. We could use the reinforcements. Is everything okay?"

There was this long silence.

Then he knew. "Tahlia?"

"I went downstairs. Saw it all." Kasha sighed. "She pulled a gun on Bullard."

"I'm sure that didn't go well."

Kasha shook her head. "No. He shot her. It's just, … well, it's sad. She was our cook. I've only known her a few days, but she seemed harmless."

"Those are the more dangerous kinds," Brandon said, pausing at the distress on her face. "Did he kill her?"

Kasha shook her head. "No. But her right arm is likely to be useless. The bullet went through her wrist. Looks like he just blew apart the bones."

"That'll be tough to heal properly."

"She needs medical help."

"What's the chance some of these gunmen are her sons?"

"I imagine both could be out there. If they find out Bullard shot their mother, it'll get ugly."

"Really? Just think. It was their mother who pulled the gun on Bullard, a man already injured, who'd been kidnapped and drugged. In his home. They'll be lucky if they have legs left to walk on before this is over," he said. "Keep in mind who's at fault here. Bullard has every right to defend himself, particularly when it's not the first attack. This is his home, and he's defending his place. We're not the bad guys here."

She let out a shaky breath. "I know. I'm just trying to remind myself that this shit happens. Unfortunately too often."

"Where is she now?"

"Bullard has her restrained and is working on her wrist and hand."

"Is he strong enough?"

Kasha shook her head. "No. But we're short on men. What's happening out here?"

"An airplane landed and was greeted with gunfire. These men did nothing, appeared to be expecting it. They hunkered down and waited."

His phone vibrated. Brandon shielded it and whispered, "Stone, what's up?"

"Levi's landed. He'll be here in a few minutes. He's coming directly into the garage."

"Then we need somebody downstairs to man that door."

"Is Kasha with you?"

"She is. Yeah. You talk to her." Brandon handed the phone to Kasha, now kneeling beside him, the wall as cover.

He half listened to the conversation, but his eyes were on the hillside and above. It didn't really surprise him that Levi would come himself and before they had even found Bullard. It took thirteen hours easily to make this trek. But how was Levi making this last leg of his trip to them? Was he coming on foot? Because nobody from here had driven out to meet him.

He waited to speak with Stone, but Kasha had hung up.

"Stone's gone already." She handed him his phone back. "But, if Levi is coming into the garage, I presume he's driving."

"Where did he get the vehicle from?"

She looked at him in surprise, glanced toward the airstrip and said, "I don't know."

They waited, and, sure enough, a plume of dust came toward the holding. "You need to hurry down, open the garage door and make sure nobody else comes in," he said in a low tone. "Can you do that?"

When she didn't answer, he gave her a sideways glance. She nodded, her face grim. "I can do that."

He felt bad sending her down alone. "I'd come, but I must keep track of these four men."

"I'll be fine," she said in an airy tone. "It's not my first war."

"Too bad," he snapped.

She froze, turned to look at him and said, "Why the bad temper?"

He shrugged. He hated to admit it to himself, but he was worried. He hated to see women in scenarios like these. She might be a warrior woman, like Ice; all indications pointed that way, just without all of Ice's firsthand experience. Yet he still hated sending Kasha into something dangerous.

She chuckled. "Look at that. You're starting to care, and we've only just met." Laughing softly, she disappeared down below.

He grinned, loving the banter. He could care … there was definitely something between them. She'd come to him just now, not the others. She was also a stunner. That she could handle herself in this situation added to the attraction.

That she'd been bothered by Tahlia's actions and subsequent shooting showed she had heart—that was important in this business.

Determined not to let her distract him, he studied and watched. The vehicle came around the corner toward the garage, and the four closest invaders got up and raced toward the holding. Instantly Brandon dropped a line of fire in front of them. The men roared and backed up to where they had been before, searching the wall for him. No way they could return fire. He was fully hidden behind the stone wall. He watched as they put their heads together once again.

From the opposite side, he could hear more gunfire. He presumed Merk was doing the same thing to keep the men on his side away from the oncoming vehicle. Stone too. All the invaders were rushing toward the garage entrance to try to stop the vehicle from coming in. Not happening ...

Just as Brandon had figured they would be smart about their lives, the men on his side got up and ran around the building. Brandon picked up the pace and stayed with them on the roof, watching the men on the ground as they joined up with their comrades in front of Merk's position.

He joined Merk and said, "What do they think they're trying to do?"

"I don't care. But whatever they do, if they come toward us, they'll be eating our bullets." Merk turned to look at him. "That garage is open. Who's down there?"

"Kasha. Tahlia pulled a gun on Bullard too."

Merk shot him a disbelieving look. "She what?"

Brandon nodded. "Pretty stupid, huh?"

"Yeah, especially now that he's slowly coming back. He got taken once. He won't be such a fool a second time."

"Apparently Bullard shot her in the hand. Caused quite

a bit of damage. Now Bullard's patching her up. She's been tied to a chair, so the chances of her pointing a second gun at him are next to none."

Just as the vehicle came into view, the men on the ground opened fire. Someone from the vehicle returned fire. Even so the invaders raced toward the garage. Brandon shot and snapped one man's hand holding a machine gun and popped another in the knee. He took out another who was lining up in his direction. With Merk working beside him, they steadily dropped all eight men. One dead, seven down.

He turned to look at Merk and said, "I don't think Bullard's got a medical clinic open, does he?"

On the other end of the holding's roof, they could hear Stone working his magic. "Why would they still try to charge even though they know we are up here?"

"I don't know. Maybe they saw something in the jeep that made them panic."

"Or they thought it was their men, and they were throwing cover shots so they could run in."

"Until they saw Levi and afterward shots were fired from the jeep." Brandon nodded. "That's likely what happened. They were expecting the vehicle to be full of their own men. Not more of us." He glanced down at the injured invaders, but nobody moved. "We still have to deal with them."

"I suggest we get somebody in the village to come and get their vermin," Merk said in a cold voice. "I bet Bullard knows exactly who to call."

Suddenly Stone roared.

Merk and Brandon stared at each other. With none of the men below capable of mounting an attack any longer, Brandon and Merk headed to Stone.

He was cursing. "One of them goddamn scraped me,"

he roared. There was a burn mark on his shoulder, but it had only grazed him, and that was what counted.

Brandon grinned. Stone was just pissed because it stung like a bitch.

Merk looked over the edge and sure enough, Stone's four invaders were dead. "Was that all you?"

Stone shook his head. "Whoever was in the vehicle heard me yell when I got stung. That was it. They went down like ants on a log."

Merk nodded. "What do you want to bet Ice came too?"

Stone's face lit up. "Now that would be like Ice," he said in satisfaction. "She doesn't let anybody pop her friends." Stone asked Brandon and Merk, "Did you leave any alive?"

Brandon shrugged. "It seemed pointless to kill them if I didn't have to."

Suddenly there was a round of gunfire from where they'd left the first eight invading men. Brandon raced back to see somebody running up the hill toward the airstrip. All the injured men had been shot in the head.

Merk joined him and said, "He killed his own men?"

Stone's voice was hard. "If you don't take him down, that asshole will come back. He'll also take out the plane."

The running man dropped to his knee and started firing. "Obviously Ice left somebody in charge of the plane." There was return fire, and the gunman was thrown back off his feet, rolled down the hill and didn't move again.

"Damn. That doesn't leave anyone here to question," Brandon said.

"Yes, but now we don't have to bother calling the medic," Merk said, then added with a hard edge, "I sure as hell hope they have an undertaker around here. Burying these guys in this ground will be a bitch."

Chapter 7

K ASHA STOOD INSIDE the open garage as they barreled forward, coming to a screeching halt. She stared at the occupants for a moment and then her face lit up. "Levi and Ice. Man, the bodies drop every time you show up."

Ice hopped out, but she was still battle ready, fully armed and spinning around, looking for more enemies. Kasha watched as Ice swept her way back outside to see if any of the men who had been shot were on the move. Levi smiled at Kasha and raced out behind Ice. Two other men were in the back of the vehicle.

She nodded and said, "Rhodes, is that you?"

"Hey, Kasha." Rhodes pointed to the guy beside him as they got out and said, "This is Flynn."

She smiled at the second man who returned a lazy grin—the kind deadly to all women—before he and Rhodes disappeared behind Levi and Ice, all checking the outside perimeter of the fortress.

That was it. She was once again alone in the garage. She made her way to the open door and took a quick look outside. Four dead men were on the right, and she had no idea how many were around the corner. She couldn't leave with the garage open, with her friends still outside, with the cabinets full of weapons. Nor could she leave Bullard without a front line of defense. She waited.

Finally Ice returned, laughing and talking to Levi at her side. She walked over and gave Kasha a hug. "Not exactly the nicest greeting in the world. Please tell me Bullard's okay."

Kasha smiled. "Bullard is Bullard. Our cook pulled a gun on him. Unfortunately for her, Bullard decided he'd had enough of being attacked."

"Did he kill her?" Levi's tone was casual, but his gaze was not. It was extremely intent and world-weary.

"No, he shot her in the hand."

"That's what I would have expected," Ice said casually. She walked toward the door. "This is a hell of a place you've got here."

"You mean a hell of a place Bullard's got here." Kasha looked back at the open doors. "I don't really want to leave the garage door open." She pointed to the cabinets. "Every one of these is full of weapons."

Levi and Ice opened the padlocks up and started to whistle. "Wow. Look at that firepower."

"I know. That's what we mean. Arms dealing. Maybe an arms depot is more like it."

The garage filled as everybody but Harrison came in. She glanced around and asked Brandon, "Where's Harrison?"

"He's standing guard on the rooftop in case anybody else comes out of the woodwork."

She nodded. "That's smart." With everybody laughing and greeting each other, she closed the big garage doors under Ice's watchful eyes. Kasha then led the way to Bullard who was now sitting and looking more alert than she had seen him since his return.

Tahlia, on the other hand, was tied to a chair, looking like she could faint from the pain.

Ice walked over to Tahlia and looked at the hand. She

didn't say a word to the woman. She turned to Bullard and said, "Have you got someone coming to collect her?"

Bullard nodded. "What passes for law enforcement in the area is on its way."

Ice nodded. "She'll need a medic."

"Hey, I patched her up. You want to help her, go right ahead. But she needs surgery, and her hand is still likely to be useless."

Ice didn't say anything. She turned her back on the woman and walked over to Bullard. He grinned and opened his arms as she stepped in for a hug. Kasha watched in quiet amazement. Bullard had had several relationships since she'd known him, but nothing compared to what he had had with Ice.

Kasha then glanced at Levi and saw he was unconcerned. He was watching all the computer equipment as the security cameras showed various scenes from around the holding.

"You've got great bones in this place here," he said. "But then, trust you, Bullard, to pick one so far away."

"I thought I'd found a prize. Not sure what I've got now."

"We'll help you to stabilize this." Levi shook hands with Bullard and smiled. "By the way, left our return flight open-ended with your pilot."

Bullard nodded.

"Still, it's not like you to get blindsided like you did."

"I'm more pissed at myself than anything. I hadn't seen any other weapons here. We hadn't had time to do a full inventory. I hired Tahlia from the village to do some cooking for us. But of course, she couldn't resist the urge to turn against me."

Kasha turned to Tahlia. "Why did you do that?" she

asked in English this time.

With pain in her voice, Tahlia said, "My sons, ... my sons, ... don't kill them ..."

Kasha stared at her in sadness. "I'm sorry. Somebody came from the village and shot down the attacking men like dogs. They could have lived. But somebody from their team put a bullet in every one of their heads."

Tahlia's heart was reflected in her expression and was clearly breaking. She started to cry.

Kasha squatted down in front of her and said, "I don't know for sure that your sons were out there."

Tahlia started to shake. "I told them to leave it alone. I told them to not run with that gang."

"What gang and what were they doing?"

"They thought they could be fighters, like so many other young men. They could go around the world and do things," she sobbed. "But what they saw as a difference, it wasn't a good one. All they saw was the money and that these men walked tall and carried weapons. They wanted that. But they were just boys. Once they were part of them, I had to do what they said or else they'd punish my sons." Then she broke into uncontrollable sobs.

Levi stepped forward. "I'll take someone to check on all the dead out there before somebody collects them."

Kasha turned back to Tahlia and asked, "What are their names and how old are they?"

Tahlia had a hard time stopping the sobs, but she managed most of the information. "They're twenty-two and twenty-six. Mohammed is the older one, and Aziz is my baby."

Levi nodded, looked to Ice and said, "You want to come?"

Ice nodded. "Let's see what we've got." To Kasha, she said, "We'll take photos."

As the two disappeared, Kasha hoped at least one of the woman's sons was alive.

Bullard sighed. "What else was I supposed to do when she pulled a gun on me? Especially after poisoning me in the first place."

"At least you didn't kill her," Stone said. "But, if her sons are dead, she will wish you had killed her too."

There wasn't a whole lot anyone could say to that. The facts of life were, people died. And, in war, they died all the time. No parent should ever have to bury their own child. But it happened way too often.

All too soon Levi and Ice returned. Without speaking a word, Levi showed Tahlia the photos of the seventeen dead men on the property.

Tahlia's wails confirmed she had lost both her boys.

Kasha was torn, but she left the woman to mourn alone.

With the arrival of Levi and Ice, the entire dynamic of the holding shifted. Kasha watched in amazement as Bullard stepped into line too. He might have groused, but he didn't argue. When Ice hugged him again, he beamed like a little boy. Kasha smiled, loving to see that side of him. She loved to see the relationships between him and his friends.

Aside from Tahlia's weeping, relative peace reigned until shortly after 11:00 p.m.—when the military arrived, two hours later than expected. They were still making plans, drinking coffee and stuffing themselves at 2:00 a.m. The military had collected all the dead men, shipping Tahlia out first after taking her statement. Then they took statements from Bullard, Kasha and Levi's team. By the time most of the military left shortly after three, Kasha was exhausted to the bone. She wanted to lie down and sleep, but it didn't look like the rest of this group was even ready to slow down. Not with a few military guys still hanging around. She'd never seen anything like it. Except maybe Bullard's own men when they were geared up for missions. But this was a different Bullard than she'd seen before. Still groggy from the drugs, he was frustrated at some residual memory loss and his inability to grasp details.

"It will come back. Give it a chance. You know what those drugs are like," Ice scolded.

"*Humph.*" He shot her a look. "Doesn't mean I have to like it."

"Doesn't mean you have to act like a two-year-old either," she said in exasperation.

Silence filled the room. Nobody else would have dared speak to Bullard like that. But Ice had a way. Bullard stared at her for a long moment, and then he chuckled. His chuckles soon turned to huge guffaws rolling throughout the room. Everybody else relaxed and grinned.

Ice shook her head. "See? Exactly what I mean." She turned back to the two remaining sergeants. They were still taking statements and had yet to take all the photos they needed.

Kasha sighed and went to make a pot of coffee.

Ice, Bullard and Levi were preparing a plan for approaching the village. With so many dead, it was hard to say what the mood would be like there. If these dead men had been terrorizing the village, then its citizens could be relieved. But, if they'd all lived there, been a part of that community, there would be many devastated families at the deaths of these men. The thing was, nobody knew which way it would go.

Including the military, talking of a reconnaissance mission through the town to test the waters. Not only did they need to know what the mood of the villagers was, they needed to know if more men were gathering for another attack. There were sixteen dead men, seventeen if you included the one on the hillside. But most of them hadn't been killed by Bullard's men. Whoever was the final shooter at the tarmac, up at the top by the airstrip, was long gone.

Levi and Ice had gone up to look. On the way they had taken out two new attackers and thought they saw one more. But there had been no sign of him when they returned. Their focus had been getting back to the holding.

Kasha had been running data for hours since the military had first shown up. She had notes and a scratch pad beside her as she continuously searched the names from the bank accounts associated with the gunrunners. Bullard had some of his IT men back at the main holding helping out too. Kasha wasn't sure she trusted the military. Not that these guys from the local village were any better so far. It was a crap shoot out here. And, although she understood some of the language, these two sergeants mostly spoke a dialect she didn't understand. That made her much more uneasy. Now she knew how the others had felt about Tahlia.

Kasha had had a more empathetic attitude. But only slightly.

"Kasha and I should drive to the village alone. We will be viewed as less threatening," Ice said. "We can get a feel for the land. Talk to some of the locals."

"What's your cover?" Brandon asked. "After all the shootings, the villagers will be extremely wary."

"No store there, right?"

Everybody shook their heads.

"Doesn't appear to be. That doesn't mean they don't have supplies we can buy," Kasha piped up. "That's quite common in this area."

Ice nodded. "I can't say I'm surprised, but we do need a cover."

"You can come in from the other end of town," Brandon suggested. "Ask for instructions to come up here."

Ice looked at him and frowned. "As if we're visitors?"

"Say you are applying for work and had been called in for an interview."

She nodded thoughtfully. "Although I'm not sure exactly what kind of job position I might be coming for." Bullard snickered. "Whatever position you want, you know you can have."

She reached over, patted him on the knee and said, "Not happening."

"He hasn't married you yet," Bullard said with a smirk. "There's always a place for you here."

There was a hard bang as Levi's chair came down on four legs. He gave Bullard a sideways look.

"What you mean is, I haven't said yes yet." Ice laughed.

Bullard broke out chuckling. "If looks could kill, Levi would have pinned me to the floor already, out for the count."

"Nah, he knows where my heart lies." She hopped to her feet, turned to look at the others and said, "Kasha's coming with me. We'll go all the way around, approach from the village as if looking for instructions on how to get here to Bullard's holding. We'll talk to the women. See if anybody is sympathetic. We'll also get a head count for the villagers if we can. I'm wondering if somebody else should come."

"It's not a case of *should* come," Levi said in a hard voice.

"Somebody is definitely going with you."

She slanted him a look and said, "I wasn't looking for protection."

He stood, shoved his hands into his back pockets and said, "I wasn't offering."

It was a tone of voice that normally nobody would have crossed. But Ice just laughed. Her laughter was so young and happy that Kasha had to wonder.

Ice nodded. "In that case, Levi, you're looking for work too."

"As if."

"So what's your cover then?" Ice challenged.

"You picked me up in Djougou as a driver," he said, his voice still hard, brooking no argument. From anyone. "You were trying to get to Bullard's place."

She raised an eyebrow and nodded. "That's not bad." She asked the group at large, "Why would Kasha and I be coming in together?"

Kasha piped up, "Because Bullard arranged for us to arrive on the same day."

"Why?" Ice asked.

"Because he only arrived a few days ago. He didn't want anybody any earlier."

Levi nodded. "We can make that work." He turned to Ice and said, "Get changed."

She glanced down at her camouflage pants and matching shirt and nodded. "I guess I have to look a little less military, don't I?"

"Speaking of which," Sergeant Reuben said, "I don't think you should go alone."

She turned to look at him. "That's what our conversation was just about. I won't be going alone."

"I should come with you."

She shook her head. "That'll defeat the purpose." She motioned at him and his outfit. "You're obviously military. That'll send everybody into silent mode. We wouldn't get anyone to talk to us."

"I can come in another vehicle," he announced. "A lot of blood has been shed already."

"Absolutely. And you can do what you need to do for your line of inquiry. But let me go in first so I can talk to the locals without that threat of military power behind me."

He considered that and said, "I'll come in half an hour behind you."

She gave him a hard look and said, "Fine." She studied her watch. "It's barely 3:45. The sun won't be up until six or so. I say we take a three-hour nap." She turned to Kasha. "We leave at seven."

Kasha turned to Bullard. Technically he was her boss. He smiled and nodded. "Ice will look after you."

"I hardly need to be looked after," she said in exasperation. "But it's still your call."

"I am temporarily unable to take command. And, in my absence, it will always be Ice and Levi who handle everything."

She raised her eyebrows at that. "Now that's a hell of a friendship."

He nodded. "One borne of a lot of years of bloodshed. I trust them both with my life. You can too."

BRANDON DIDN'T LIKE the idea of being left behind. "I'd like to come too."

Ice turned to look at him. "What would your cover be?"

she joked.

"Well, if Levi is driving, then I'm along for protection and will be the lookout, right?"

Levi nodded. "You can come."

The others started to holler.

"I don't want to leave Bullard's holding defenseless," Ice said. "So you guys decide while Kasha and I get in a nap."

AT SUNRISE, ICE crossed into a small room, grabbing one of the bags on her way. Kasha looked at her own outfit, decided she was good to go, but she wasn't going without weapons. At a cabinet she pulled out her pistol, checked for rounds, grabbed a clip, popped it in her pocket and tucked the handgun into her waistband, pulling her dark T-shirt over it. A few minutes later, now changed into jeans and a white T-shirt, Ice joined her, pulling out a gun from the cabinet too.

"Bullard, nice of you to buy something so fully stocked," Ice said in admiration. "I have to admit that I'm jealous as hell."

"You know the military will confiscate ninety percent of it, don't you?"

She laughed. "Ninety percent of what they can find."

Brandon joined them. He gave them a quick once-over, nodded and said, "Let's go."

They piled into the one truck that hadn't been to the village yet. Levi took position as the official driver, with Levi and Kasha seated up front, Ice sitting between them. Brandon jumped into the bed and sat up against the window between them.

"There have to be other vehicles abandoned some-where," Kasha said. "These men didn't walk that whole way."

"How far is it to the village?" Ice asked.

"Three to four miles," Kasha said. "They could have walked, but I doubt they did. Almost everyone here is lazy as hell." Then she laughed. "That's not true. I certainly would have preferred driving instead of walking."

"Those from the village are likely scouting for the vehicles and the men," Ice added.

Kasha nodded. "We could be walking into a trap too. Did you consider that?"

"Absolutely, that's why we have another vehicle coming behind us about ten minutes later," Ice said. She glanced at Brandon sitting behind them in the truck bed, the window open between them. "Besides, Brandon's here. He's hell on wheels with a rifle, a hand gun, a knife and in hand-to-hand combat."

Brandon flashed his white teeth at Kasha. "You'll be fine."

Kasha sniffed and raised her nose in the air. "I didn't say I wasn't fine. I just wondered if anyone seriously wasn't expecting the village to be aware of what happened here?"

"Well," Ice said, "let's just hope nobody ran home and told everybody a blond Amazon woman is here."

"But that doesn't mean somebody isn't on the hills with a spyglass keeping track."

"Absolutely. I would expect them to. If they are any kind of mercenaries, they should not only have backup, but they should have backup to that backup."

"Part of the reason for that is they'll betray each other," Brandon said.

Ice smiled. "True enough."

With Levi driving and Brandon sitting in the open truck

bed, riding shotgun, they drove toward the airstrip. "There's a road behind the airstrip," Kasha said. "You can come around and make it an eight-mile trip instead of a four."

Levi didn't say a word. He just followed instructions. Brandon didn't let his gaze stop moving. The last thing they wanted was to be picked off by a sharpshooter. That was one of the hardest things to avoid. With his eyes peeled for enemies, everyone remained quiet until they approached the village. Buildings lining the roadway had clear plastic coverings on several windows on either side, and even more had no coverings at all. That made Brandon a little nervous, and he wished he was in the front, but he did what he could from where he was. As they drove slowly into the village, there was no sign of anyone. That weird creepy feeling crawled up his neck again.

He might not see anyone, but they were being watched. He was sure of it. He poked his head forward into the cab. When Kasha turned to look at him, he asked, "Can you see anything?"

"No, but I can feel it. Every instinct I have is telling us to get the hell out of here."

Levi's voice was calm and collected as he said, "I hear you. But we need information first." He pulled up to a large building and parked. He stood beside the truck, leaning insolently against the side. Brandon hopped out. He left his weapon leaning against the side of the truck beside Levi as the women exited and walked a little way away. As if having nothing to do with them. Brandon glanced at them, but the two were talking with their heads together. He didn't know if it was for show or if the two women did have something to say.

Up ahead were two older women sitting on the edge of a

doorstep. Ice spoke quickly, using lots of hands. But the women just looked at her blankly. As Brandon watched, Kasha stepped forward and translated.

The women looked from one to the other and started talking. They pointed toward the other end of the village.

Ice smiled and nodded as she crouched down in front of the two women.

"Do you ever wonder what she says at times like these?" Brandon asked.

"The thing about Ice is, she always knows what to say in any given situation. I'd as soon lift a rifle and ask somebody to speak. In her case she gets gentle and can talk to women and men. She understands people."

Kasha spun suddenly as if hearing something. A younger woman came out of a small home. She was crying and holding her baby in her hands.

Brandon feared this wouldn't end well. He didn't know who she was, but, with as many dead men as they had found so far, some backlash was expected.

With Kasha interpreting, Ice spoke to the young woman.

She was almost beside herself with grief. They talked for a long time. But Levi never showed any impatience. He leaned against the truck and waited. Brandon walked around to the passenger side and waited there for five minutes and then walked around back again. No other sounds came from the village. As Brandon approached Levi, Levi's low voice said, "Two at nine o'clock."

"Saw them."

Casually Brandon leaned against the truck, shuffling so he could stare directly at the two men approaching.

They carried machine guns above their shoulders—very familiar-looking weapons.

Brandon had left his leaning against the truck, but it was only a hand's grip away. Levi turned and studied the two men and then deliberately turned his back on them. Brandon watched the anger ripple across their faces, and a spate of some language streamed at them. Levi ignored them, but his body was tense, waiting for the action.

When Kasha saw the men approaching Brandon and Levi, she raced toward them, calling out in their language. They turned to look at her. She reached them, speaking rapidly as she motioned toward Levi and Brandon, and more explanations ensued. Finally it seemed like everybody calmed down. Only Brandon remained tense inside and out. He didn't quite understand what was going on. But the machine guns were now slung on the men's backs. That he understood very well.

Kasha walked over to him and said, "They said they have had many strangers here recently. Men with war on their minds. No one here is safe. The villagers don't like strangers, and we need to leave."

"We're happy to leave. Did you ask for directions to Bullard's place?"

"Yes. Got them. But he said it wasn't Bullard's place. Before you say anything, I explained Bullard bought it and had the papers to prove it. I also said Bullard had no intention of disrupting their way of life. He had hoped to hire some people from the village."

Brandon asked in low tones, "Do you think there's anything else to learn?"

She turned back toward Ice who even now was talking to somebody yet again. Kasha flashed him a smile and said, "I've got to go." She ran toward Ice.

Having stepped away, the two local males leaned against

one of the closest buildings, watching.

They glared at Brandon. He glared right back. He wasn't sure how to defuse the situation. Finally Ice and Kasha returned casually to the truck and climbed inside. Brandon jumped into the back. He made a point of keeping his rifle with him. They drove slowly through the village. Now that everyone had spoken to several men and women, other people started to show up on their doorsteps, watching as Levi carefully maneuvered them along the unpaved dirt road through the village.

Brandon knew dozens more were watching from behind walls. He didn't blame them. This truck was full of strangers, and the townspeople's world had probably shifted from bad to worse in the last few weeks. Particularly last night. It wasn't his fault those villagers wouldn't be coming home, but Brandon felt he was partly responsible.

They needed to know who it was who had betrayed them all. But Brandon doubted anybody would believe him. The fact the villagers had somebody in their midst who had turned around and killed their own men, well, unfortunately Brandon had seen way too much of that in the world.

As soon as they were through town, Kasha turned to look at Brandon. "You okay back there?"

"I'm okay. What about you?"

She nodded. "That was tough. That woman was looking for the father of her child. He went out with one of the groups last night, and he hasn't come home."

"Chances are he won't be coming home—ever. And of course nobody mentioned guns or gun deals, correct?"

She gave a hard laugh. "No, I'm not sure the women even know. The men certainly weren't talking."

"They never do," Ice added. "They never do."

Chapter 8

KASHA WAS STILL shivering inside even though Levi
drove them home. It was not so much the shock or the
fear of the last twenty minutes, but just hearing and seeing
the results of all that shooting earlier—the personal losses—
well, it was devastating. They hadn't killed all those villagers,
but how could they prove that to those left behind? She
didn't know. Then this was weapons dealing. What the hell
did anybody expect?

Things like this just went bad from the beginning.

It made her long for a normal life back home, whatever
that meant. It seemed so long ago that she had lived that life.
Since working for Bullard, her life had been an ever-
changing landscape, and, in the last few months, she'd
wanted something different. Only she had no clue what that
was. What else would she do? Maybe she could go back to
school, but she had no idea what she wanted to study. She
had money, after all; she'd had little to spend it on over the
years here, and Bullard was very generous. The truth was, if
she wanted to get a degree, she could. But it had to be
meaningful. It had to be worth the years of effort, and it had
to give her something she wanted at the end. The trouble
was, she didn't know what she wanted. Yet she had this void
inside.

She admired Ice. That woman was incredible, but was

that what Kasha wanted for herself? It was tough. So much death. Seeing that woman with her baby, … that had to be devastating for a mother. To know what had happened made it that much worse.

She tried to figure out a way forward. "I guess the military will take this over and find out what happened to the men," she said out loud.

"Not necessarily," Ice said. "I'm not sure they weren't part of that group."

"What makes you think that?"

"The soldiers never once asked where the weaponry was that the gunrunners had sold," Ice said. "Did anybody else notice that? It's as if they already knew. The only way they could have known is if they've been there."

For the rest of the way home Kasha contemplated the ramifications of their trip. "Do you think they know we're onto them?"

"That's why Flynn and Rhodes haven't shown themselves. They are following the soldiers." Ice gave her a grim smile. "We need to know what they are up to. My guess is, no good."

"How does a country run with that level of corruption?"

"A lot of countries have the same issues. They steal thousands to millions of dollars from companies, government coffers and anywhere else they can rob. Nobody is the wiser because no watchdog is keeping track of it. There's nobody to look over their shoulder, or, if there is, often they're just paid to look the other way."

"I guess honor is a thing of the past."

"I don't think it is," Ice said. "I just think there's less of it. A lot more assholes are running the world. They were always there, but it's more about a balance. Finding who and what works, not just in a relationship but also for a government."

Kasha laughed. "Oh, my goodness, that's awesome."

Ice shot her a devilish look. "It boils down to people, relationships, communication. Don't forget we've been doing this for a long time." As she returned her gaze to the road, the windshield exploded. Both women screamed, but Levi kept driving forward.

Kasha twisted to look over the back of the seat, and, sure enough, the back window had been shattered. "Brandon?" she screamed.

"I'm okay," he yelled. "Stay down."

Kasha lay on the bench seat as Ice was jammed down in the footwell on her phone. "We were just shot at. We're fine but coming in fast and hard." She dropped the phone beside her and, with weapon in hand, popped up and searched their surroundings.

"It had to have been a sharpshooter but from where?" Kasha asked. "There's no place to hide."

"Camouflaged, lying flat on the ground," Levi said. "It doesn't take much to have a small stand, enough to lift up for beautiful long-distance shots like that."

"Well, I hope he doesn't get another chance."

Levi didn't bother answering. He shifted gears, turned the corner and then the stronghold was ahead of them. They raced forward at full speed.

"Don't you want to slow down for this?" Kasha asked.

"Hell no," Ice answered for Levi. "Hold on. We're going to brake, and we're going to brake hard."

In another thirty seconds they peeled down the road toward the garage. Harrison and Bullard streamed out of garage, rifles at the ready to ward off any attack. Levi drove in and hit the brakes hard, turned the wheel and spun the vehicle around so it faced the way they came. Kasha barely understood what had happened, and suddenly the garage door was down, and they were safe.

Bullard raced over. "Kasha, are you all right?"

She sat up, a little shakily, brushed the glass off her clothing and gave him a smile. "I am. Levi is a hell of a driver."

Bullard nodded. "He is at that. Like Ice is a hell of a pilot."

Kasha watched as Ice helped herself to one of the semi-automatics from the cabinets. Then she grabbed the ammunition she needed and loaded the clips. She turned around and said, "Levi and Brandon are going out. I'm going up. The military is behind us."

Bullard, with Ice and Kasha right behind him, ran to the rooftop walkway. There they could see the plume of a second vehicle way off in the distance.

"That's the military in front, right? So who is coming behind the military then?" Kasha asked Ice.

"Stone and Merk."

Kasha did a head count and realized that only left Harrison with Bullard—not many people here while they did their recon in the village. At least all were converging back again here. She did a quick lap around the top of the wall, watching for any other disturbances from any direction. The last thing she wanted was to have her attention on one corner and allow somebody else to sneak around another. Sure enough, when she came around the next corner, she saw two men crawling along the ground.

She called out to Ice and Bullard, "Two coming up behind us."

Bullard was already there. He still looked weak, but she knew him better than to believe he'd lie down while everybody else worked to defend his newest holding. He stood beside her, raised his rifle and shot at the ground in front of the men. Dirt flew in their faces. The two men bolted backward. She looked at Bullard and said, "Was that just a warning shot?"

He nodded. "They get one chance," he said grimly. "If they choose to not see it as that and try again, I won't hold back."

Considering what these men were likely to do if they got into the place, she had to agree. She, Bullard and Ice stayed in place for another twenty minutes with no new movement on the grounds. Then the men disappeared into the hills and kept on going. When the first vehicle showed up clearer in the distance, Kasha pointed out the plume of dust. But Bullard had already seen it. "Hopefully those are the military. Our guys should be right behind them." He frowned. "Or more men thinking to come back after that shipment."

"If the military is involved in the gunrunning, like Ice is afraid they are, we already gave them all the information they needed with our interviews, didn't we?"

"No," he said cheerfully. "I already sent the documents off to people I trust. They're considering it from their end. It doesn't matter what these guys try to do. They're small fish. They have been paid either to stay silent or to help smooth the process. There will be a penalty for their treachery. It's the bosses above them we need."

Brandon walked up behind them. "We've got word of an approaching vehicle."

"Good. We're keeping track of that plume in the distance. Wondering which group is arriving first," Kasha said.

"Bullard, why don't you go downstairs and lie down," Brandon said.

Bullard shot him a hard look. "I'm doing just fine."

Brandon nodded. "You might be. But nobody's downstairs handling communications."

Bullard looked torn, so Kasha took the decision away from him. "You know it'll take two of us to keep things running smoothly," she said. "Brandon, are you okay to handle this here?"

He looked almost as insulted as Bullard had. "Of course I am."

She chuckled and said, "Bullard, come on. Let's go."

He shrugged and let himself be led downstairs. She was surprised but happy with Brandon's suggestion. Bullard looked a little on the frail side and still had to be throwing off those unidentified drugs that Tahlia and the villagers had given him. It was a fight that would require time. Downstairs they realized it was a good thing they had come. They'd missed several important messages.

Bullard made the return calls. "Sorry, Konrad. I wasn't here for your call. What's up?" He put the phone on Speaker.

"We have information on the group selling the guns." Konrad's deep voice filled the room. "We need to set up a sting to make sure we catch these men. We're highly suspicious there could be military police involved too."

"Well, I can give you the names of the two just here. I'm pretty sure they are involved. They also followed a reconnaissance mission that we sent into the local village. To see what was going on. I'm expecting them back at any moment."

"Are you thinking they're involved, or are you thinking

they've been taken out?" Konrad asked.

Kasha listened in on the conversation. She winced and said in a low tone, "I can see both happening."

Bullard gave her a long look and then said, "I agree. I suspect they were involved."

She heard the withdrawn breath on the other end of the phone. "Okay, I'm on my way. I'm sending down four men to sort this out." Konrad rattled off the names. "Don't let anybody else in there."

"Wasn't planning on it. But they better identify themselves as soon as they are visible. We had armed invaders last night. I've got my men all around this place. Then the two women who went to the village on my behalf first thing this morning were shot at. If one of those bullets had hit either of them, I would have gone in there and taken out that village. You know that, right?"

"We don't raze anything to the ground just because we're angry. Let's make sure we get the people shooting, not the innocents."

Bullard nodded, his tone terse. "Like I said, make sure they identify themselves." He hung up. He glanced at his watch and said, "It'll be at least four hours until Konrad's men arrive."

Kasha rubbed her temple. "So, stand watch until then?"

"More or less. But I suspect we've got another attack coming regardless." He looked around. "We'll need food. Are there any rations?"

She chuckled. "Well, there's food. Although not much, but I'll find something for us to eat in a pinch."

"The men are all good cooks too. If you need a hand, just shout."

She made her way to the kitchen. There were huge

stoves, both wood and electric, plus large fridges and coolers. The kitchen had been modernized and should have been well stocked. But, because they hadn't had a chance to do even a basic shopping trip, it wasn't. She did an inventory. Found lots of bread. A whole ham. As soon as she saw that, she shrugged. "Sandwiches it is."

She set out to make a couple dozen sandwiches. She wasn't sure how many people she would have to feed, but given the number of men so far, she figured there wasn't enough for two sandwiches each. Salad fixings were in the fridge, but they lacked substance. Regardless she'd serve it anyway. She found some eggs, which she hard-boiled, and cooked some potatoes. She was humming away in the kitchen, finishing off the potato salad, when a hand slapped over her mouth, and an arm choked her windpipe.

Her heel went up and crunched down on her attacker's foot. She realized she was up against steel-toed boots but managed to get her teeth clear, and she bit down hard on the fingers at her mouth. The man roared and smacked her on the side of the head. But she was free. She turned and caught him in the jaw with a high kick that snapped his head backward. She was on him in an instant. It took another thirty seconds to subdue him using some of the strongholds Bullard had shown her—certain nerve centers she could press to knock out a man. Thank God she knew them.

Shakily she stood and stared at the intruder. "How the hell had he gotten in?" That was what worried her the most. And if there was one …

She pulled out her cell phone and called Bullard but got no answer. She sent a message to Brandon. **Attacked in kitchen. No answer from Bullard.**

She got a text right back. **Coming.**

She looked around the kitchen for something to tie up the intruder. But there was damn little available. Using a kitchen knife, she cut off the lower part of his T-shirt. With that she bound his hands behind him and then his feet and then tied the two together behind him. It still worried her that he might not have come on his own.

Had his partner gone after Bullard? With her weapon in her hand, she moved quickly to the war room.

Bullard was arguing fiercely with somebody. Then she heard a hard smack. She realized some asshole had hit Bullard across the face. Inside her stomach churned, and her anger boiled. She was more than fed up with these assholes. As she peered around the corner, she caught sight of Brandon standing at the other entrance to the room, his face equally grim as he studied what was going on inside the huge central room.

He caught her eye and held up two fingers. She assumed that meant there were two men. Then he held up three for a long moment. Then dropped one, then the next. *A countdown.* As soon as he dropped the final finger, he moved and fired twice. Bullard threw his hands up in the air and dropped to the floor out of the line of fire. She followed Brandon into the room. She raised her gun, found a target and pulled the trigger. Twice. Crouching low, Brandon checked to make sure there was nobody else.

Bullard called out as he rose off the floor, "There were just the two."

Brandon stood over the two dead men and smiled. "You're a good shot," he told Kasha.

Kasha stared at the two men, both sporting double bullet holes. "So are you."

He grinned, but his smile fell away as he looked at her.

"I am sorry. Life's a bitch now and again."

This was not how she'd expected her afternoon to go. She turned to Bullard. "Are you okay?"

He nodded. "With you two looking after me, I'm doing just fine." And he grinned at her.

She shook her head, looked again at the two dead men and asked, "Who's going to take out the garbage?" She glanced around, but Brandon was already gone. Bullard laughed out loud. "He's gone to see if there are any other intruders."

"Which is something I should have been thinking about."

"I'm hoping you had enough time to get some food rustled up. These guys gave me an appetite." He cracked his knuckles together, bent down, grabbed the collar of each guy and dragged them across the floor.

She watched in awe. Talk about brute strength. Bullard was like the others. He just didn't think anything of the kind of muscle he commanded. For her to move just one of those men would have been a major effort. She could've done it, but she'd have been exhausted at the end of it. She wished she knew where Brandon had gone because she should've gone after him as backup.

"Which way did they come from? Do you know?" she called after Bullard.

"From the section you came from."

"Right. That makes sense. I was attacked in the kitchen."

Bullard dropped the two men and turned to stare at her. "What?"

"I left him tied up in the kitchen."

"He's alive?" Bullard asked with a grin. "Damn, that's good. Let's go have a little talk with your visitor."

Two minutes later they were in the kitchen, and Kasha screamed in outrage. "He's gone. I left him tied up right here." She pointed. "He's gone."

Bullard shook his head and said, "Then chances are, there are more."

BRANDON DID A quick sweep of the upstairs rooms floor by floor, then came back down to the kitchen. He stopped when he saw Kasha and Bullard snapping at each other. "What's the matter?"

Kasha turned, obviously upset and said, "I left one of the intruders tied up here, but now he's gone." She raised both hands in frustration. "He couldn't get out of it on his own."

Brandon didn't say anything. He had seen some artists escape from the damnedest setups. He looked around and said, "They aren't upstairs, so we need to find out if they're on this floor and how they arrived."

"I suspect there's an entrance we don't know about," Bullard said. "As much as I really like that idea, it really pisses me off that they found it before I knew of it. That's why properties should come with decent blueprints."

Together the three searched the kitchen. At the pantry, Kasha walked in, looked around and shrugged before stepping out. "Don't know what we're trying to find. We've been through here many times, and it all looks the same."

Brandon opened the first cupboard door and whistled. "Did you see this before?"

She peered over his shoulder and gasped. "No. I didn't. We must have missed opening this one."

Instead of shelves, there was a staircase. With his weapon in front of him and Kasha behind him, they swept down the stairs to a small tunnel. There were no lights, and it was dark, but he could touch it from side to side. It was well made and appeared to be extremely old.

He glanced back to see Bullard looming behind him, his grinning teeth flashing in the dark. For men like them, this was priceless—a way to get out when under attack was huge. Brandon turned on the flashlight on his phone and picked up the pace, lightly running, racing forward. He doubted there would be any sign of the invaders, but, if they thought they still had a secret entrance, they could come back or possibly take their time getting out. The tunnel seemed to go on forever. Eventually Brandon saw a light up ahead. He figured the outer door to the tunnel was open, letting in sunlight. He shut down his cell phone and pocketed it.

As he got closer, he heard voices. He turned and held up a hand, warning the other two. He crept forward, Kasha right behind him, as he tried to listen to the conversation. She interpreted with her mouth right against his ear. "They are waiting for two more men. They heard the gunshots upstairs and assumed two of their men were gone. They're wondering now if they can wait until nightfall and move the guns to the tunnel."

He nodded and whispered, "That would make sense on their part."

It wouldn't work, but he didn't tell her that. What he wanted was to wait for the other two men to arrive and then take down all four of them. He crept another step forward. It was hard to see anything, and there was an odd reflection with the light. They stood on sand, but, at the same time, there were rocks.

The voices suddenly stopped.

Kasha grabbed his shoulder and squeezed. He froze.

Then the voices resumed.

Kasha stepped forward and whispered against his ear again, "They're arguing about the best way. The other man wants to come back inside and shoot everybody here, so they don't have to worry about it. They can just take back the fortress."

Brandon raised his eyebrows at that. It was nobody's property but Bullard's. However, in places like this, possession was often nine-tenths of the law.

The argument rose louder. Then finally one made a hard sound, and the two arguing men both fell silent again.

Brandon twisted to look at Kasha for an interpretation. She shrugged. "No solution. They're waiting for the two others."

It was nearing nine in the morning. It was sunny and bright outside as evidenced by the light filtering into the tunnel. The invaders had had trouble getting across the huge open spaces surrounding the holding last night in the dark with everybody on guard. Brandon wondered how long before they gave up now in the daylight. Then suddenly he didn't have to wonder because they were arguing yet again.

In a low tone Kasha whispered, "They've decided to come back in and take out everybody on the lower floors. They only saw Bullard and me. So they think they can take us both out and then go to the rooftop and pick off the rest one by one."

He nodded. There was no place to hide in this narrow dark tunnel. He searched the long tunnel looking for an answer to their predicament. If the two men standing outside decided to enter the tunnel, he and Kasha had no place to go. Neither did Bullard, but he was still behind them. If a defensive move wasn't an option, then he'd accept an offensive one.

Making a sudden decision, Brandon ran up to the tunnel's entrance and flattened against the wall just out of sight of the two argumentative men near the entrance.

As soon as one of the men turned to enter the tunnel, he had twisted his head slightly to talk to the man behind him.

Perfect. Brandon shot the second man in his gun hand, who had seen Brandon but couldn't react fast enough. After a second shot from Brandon, both men went down. One man screamed, and Brandon pointed the gun at his face and yelled, "Shut up."

The man was reduced to sobs as he held his injured hand against his chest. Brandon nudged him with his foot and said to Kasha, "Tell them to get up. We want to talk with them."

She translated. The man stumbled to his feet, and, sobbing quietly, he tripped over his friend and crumpled to the ground again. With Bullard keeping an eye on the first man, Brandon leaned over to check on the second. Instantly the man came off the ground and swung at him, a knife in one hand. Swearing softly, Brandon kicked at the guy's knife hand and twisted, narrowly avoiding being stabbed.

The confines of the tunnel didn't allow for much movement in the way of avoiding contact; there was just no room to maneuver. He knew Bullard and Kasha couldn't shoot in such close quarters, but Brandon hadn't spent as many hours on the streets as he had for nothing. With his feet and his fists moving hard and fast, he quickly subdued the second man, and, with a final hard upper cut to his jaw, he knocked him out cold. He stood there swearing fiercely.

Then he caught sight of the first man swinging a gun around toward Bullard. Brandon didn't wait. He pivoted and swung, dealing the gunman a hard upper right to the jaw too. The man went down in a heap at Bullard's feet. Bullard looked at Brandon in horror. "Couldn't you a least let him walk through the tunnel on his own? This way we have to carry him."

Brandon rolled his eyes. "In that case I guess it's my job."

Bullard snickered. "Nah. I got one, and you got one, but I'm going to eat whatever Kasha had time to make when we reach the kitchen." He pointed at the two injured men and said, "Interrogating them can wait. Or I'll go through that bloody fridge and haul out anything edible because I'm starved."

Brandon smirked. "You're right. You go ahead and eat while Kasha and I wait to capture the two new guys at the *kitchen* end of the tunnel."

Chapter 9

F OOD WAS A hurried affair. Now with the four prisoners safely stowed on the far side of the room, everyone grabbed sandwiches and bowls of salads, whether green or potato or both. When Ice surveyed the meal, she nodded and said, "Good, I'm glad you found the food."

Kasha turned to look at her. "You brought food with you?"

She nodded. "Somewhere around here is another box." She turned around and spotted it stacked against the back wall. She flipped open the lid and chuckled. "Maybe I shouldn't let you guys know this is here."

Bullard took one look and gave a big whoop. He grabbed the box and brought it back to the table. Between the two of them, they unloaded muffins and a large chocolate cake, several loaves of bread and large chunks of wrapped up cheese and what appeared to be the bulk of a cooked roast beef in a small cooler.

Ice shook her head. "This is just what Alfred managed to pull together at a moment's notice."

Kasha walked over, her jaw dropping. "I wish I'd realized this was all here."

"Oh, don't worry. We'll eat all the sandwiches and all this too," Ice said. Within minutes, she had the roast beef sliced, along with the bread. Kasha looked back to see all the ham sandwiches were gone. She frowned. "Surely we didn't eat that many already."

Brandon returned then. "We just did a shift change," he announced. He accepted a plate of sandwiches Kasha had held back for him. "This looks great." His gaze landed on the chocolate cake, and he grinned. "I guess I got lucky with my shift change."

"You're a smart man," Bullard said. He snatched the knife away from Ice and proceeded to cut the triple layer chocolate cake. He stopped for a moment, frowned, glanced around and then said, "I guess I should share, huh?"

Ice snickered. "Yeah, you should. Levi won't take it kindly if you eat it all."

"But he has Alfred. Nobody makes chocolate cake like him."

"And what about Dave?"

Just then Levi walked in. His eyes lit up at the cake on the table, and he put a piece on his plate along with slabs of cheese and roast beef. He walked to the end of the table and sat down. He never said a word but plowed through the food with an impressive efficiency. By the time everybody had eaten, with Ice snagging pieces of the cake for the men up on the rooftop, not a whole lot of food was left.

"How's the coffee situation?" Levi asked.

"I brought a couple packs of beans with me," Bullard said. He frowned and looked around the kitchen. "But I'll be damned if I know where they are."

Brandon and Kasha both got up and searched. Brandon found the beans, tossed them on the counter and said, "Do we have a grinder?"

Kasha knew where that was. Within minutes, they had a large pot brewing. As she studied the amount of coffee and the number of people, she realized they'd have to put on a couple pots just for everyone to get a cup. Still, this was a window into a lifestyle she hadn't expected. It was fun. Everyone working together brought a lot of camaraderie.

One could learn so much about men sharing a meal. They all looked after themselves but made sure nobody else went short. She sat down, fatigue running through her, wondering how long these guys could keep going like this. Brandon looked over at her, his gaze sharp. "Looks like you need four hours downtime."

She snorted. "I'll be lucky if I get two."

"Two it is though," Bullard said, his tone hard. "You need to go crash right now."

She shook her head. "I'll be fine."

"No, you won't," Brandon snapped. "That's when you make mistakes."

She glared at him. "Who died and made you boss?"

He brought his face forward to hers and said, "If you don't look after yourself, somebody else has to force you to."

Instead of backing down, she thrust her face so it was almost touching his. "You're not doing that. I can look after myself."

"Yeah, and how's that working out for you?"

She narrowed her gaze, hating that he could see something she hadn't wanted anybody to know. Bullard's voice cut the silence. "Brandon's right, Kasha."

She spun and looked at him. "I'm fine," she repeated.

"It doesn't matter if you're fine," Brandon said. "If you're part of a team, it's also how much energy you have to help out the others. Go take some downtime. When you come back, you'll be fresher and more help."

She didn't want to give in so easily but also knew part of

the reason she was so punchy was she was tired. Without a word, she stood and left.

Brandon glanced over at Bullard and said, "Where will she crash?"

Bullard shrugged. "There are bedrooms upstairs. We all just grabbed one. So far I have been sleeping on the god-damn stretcher."

Brandon frowned. "I don't like the idea of her being up there alone."

"Don't let her hear you say that. She's a good fighter."

"I know that. I saw her in action. But, when she's asleep, she's defenseless. That's not cool for any of us right now."

Ice stood and said, "I could use some shut-eye myself. I'll go up with her."

STILL WITH MISGIVINGS, Brandon watched the two women leave. He glanced at Levi to see him contemplating their actions too. He looked over at Brandon and said, "Two hours each?"

Brandon nodded. "Done. I'll take first watch." He stood, grabbed a cup of coffee and a muffin, and, after waiting for what he considered enough time to avoid being seen by Kasha or Ice, headed upstairs. When he followed the women's voices to find which bedroom they were in, he sat down in the hall outside. He'd be damned if he'd let anything happen to them now. They'd had just enough intruders in this massive place that made it all too likely that somebody else could still be hiding inside. And, with all the drama, no more security cameras had been emplaced. The last thing Brandon wanted was to be caught unaware.

Ten minutes into his vigil, he heard a noise at the end of

the hallway. He stood and snuck around the corner of the stone entranceway to the bedroom. All the doors were set back from the hallway, so, when closed, it gave him just barely enough space to hide. It didn't allow him a chance to look, not without peering around and showing himself. He waited, and, sure enough, he now heard footsteps.

Was it his people or someone else? The person crept closer. Just by that fact alone Brandon realized it had to be an intruder. Brandon waited. The only reason he would be coming here was if he had some idea the women were here too. Brandon waited.

He tensed his muscles and locked down, hardly breathing, his chest rising in slow controlled movements so he could let air out silently. He listened as the intruder approached. Then the intruder stopped. Brandon smiled as the barrel end of a rifle appeared.

Without hesitation Brandon grabbed the rifle, flipped the butt and hit the intruder hard in the face. The man went down and tried to get up, but the business end of the rifle was already on his throat.

Brandon said, "Oh, no, you don't. Stay right where you are." When the man made a move, Brandon shoved the weapon harder under his jaw. The man stilled.

The door behind him opened. Ice stepped out and asked, "You got him?"

"Yes. Have you got something to secure him?"

She disappeared and came back a moment later with zip ties. With Brandon holding the gunman still, she bound his hands and his feet behind him. Then she pulled out her phone and called Levi. She looked at Brandon and said, "Kasha is still asleep. If you're good here, I'll head back in and try to catch some more shut-eye."

She turned and walked back into the bedroom. He hadn't even had a chance to answer her question. So he assumed she already knew he was fine. Levi arrived minutes later. "Where did he come from?"

Brandon pointed. "I heard a noise down there."

Levi took off in that direction. Brandon cut the ties then hauled the gunman to his feet and waited for Levi to return. When he didn't come back immediately, Brandon worried there might have been a second intruder. But then Levi returned, checking every room and door. As he approached, he said, "This place is a mausoleum. It could hide a full army."

Brandon nodded. "That's half the problem."

Between them, they took the intruder downstairs, so Bullard could see he had yet another asshole in his house. Bullard took one look at his face, shook his head and said, "Tie him up with the others."

When the other four prisoners saw the newest arrival, their faces fell.

Brandon snickered. "Did you think he would mount a rescue and get you guys out of here?" He shook his head. "Not happening."

One of the men spewed out a language which Brandon didn't understand. He ignored it and proceeded to set the most recent captive on a chair. He tied him up far enough away from the others that they couldn't help each other get free. Then he sat down on another chair with the rifle across his knees. The newest prisoner just kept yelling and screaming.

Bullard came in with a cup of coffee and responded in the same language.

Brandon looked at Bullard with renewed respect. Some

of these languages were deadly hard to learn. Then again Bullard had been living in Africa for a good decade. Maybe languages were easy for him. They weren't for Brandon. He could handle English, and that was about it. But many of his teammates spoke multiple languages. It was always an asset.

When Bullard fell silent, Brandon asked, "And?"

"They're after the weapons. The delivery wasn't made this morning as planned, so they're in trouble because they've been paid for those weapons. They need to get the shipment out of here and into the other guy's hands. Otherwise they'll be killed."

Brandon winced. "Sucks to be them then, doesn't it?"

Bullard nodded. He glanced at Levi, and Brandon realized Levi had been listening in on the whole thing. Brandon rose, walking with Bullard to join Levi at the doorway. The prisoners could understand English all too well.

Brandon whispered, "Can we use that information?"

"Yes, and we need to," Levi said. "It still might not save their lives. If they've taken money and not delivered the goods, … well, some people have a very long memory."

"Unless we can pick up the buyers," Brandon said quietly. Not that he had any interest in saving these men's lives. They were gunrunners. Risks were involved. Brandon also understood that life here was hard. People did whatever they could to make a living. At the same time, they didn't have to come after everyone in Bullard's holding.

"They also said," Bullard continued, "the new delivery date is now Tuesday, supposedly first thing tomorrow morning. And, if they don't get there with the weapons this time, the buyers will raze the village."

"Now that I believe," Brandon said. He frowned at Bullard. "Not sure what you've got in mind, but, if you're ready to make peace with the innocent villagers, this could be a way to turn this around, so they look up to you and won't steal from you and will effectively be your loyal spies in the area."

Bullard turned that hard gaze on Brandon. "Explain."

Brandon cast a questioning glance at Levi, and, seeing his nod, he returned his attention to Bullard. "It's easy. Even though the exchange is set for tomorrow, you know the buyers are already in the area. After all, they were supposed to get their weapons this morning to begin with. For the sake of this deal and for the innocent villagers' lives, we set a trap, and, when the men come to raze the village or we flush them out—whichever comes first—we take them out. The weapons don't get into their hands. The villagers aren't killed for being innocent bystanders."

Bullard seemed to toss the ideas around in his head. Finally he nodded and said, "I like it." He glanced over at Brandon and said, "Set it up." Then he turned and left.

Brandon looked at Levi and said, "What?"

"Now you did it," Levi said, chuckling. "Time to step up, Brandon. Bullard has high standards." He took off after Bullard, whistling lightly in the air.

Inside Brandon swore. Now what the hell had he gotten himself into?

Yet he had to admit this was something he was good at. He sat down to make plans at the kitchen table, facing his prisoners, the rifle atop the table. Even though Brandon had limited money and limited men, he had lots of weapons. He'd take those odds any day.

Chapter 10

KASHA WOKE UP slowly. She lay in the darkness wondering where she was. Directly in front of her, Ice lay sleeping. Every part of Kasha's body hurt. It was all coming back to her now. She checked her watch and winced. Instead of two hours, she'd been out for three hours. Someone should have woken her up. Crap. She hated not pulling her weight. Quietly, so as to not wake Ice, Kasha got up and made her way out to the hall. She found Levi sitting on the floor outside their door with a notepad in his hand. He glanced up and smiled. "Feel better now?"

"Yes, thank you," she whispered. She loved the thought he was watching over Ice while she slept. Kasha walked down the hall to the bathroom and used the facilities. This house was huge, with at least twenty bathrooms in it. If she'd thought about it, she would have grabbed one of the rooms with an en suite bath. She vowed to change her location tonight. If they were still here then.

With everything not settled here yet, Kasha wondered when the plane was scheduled to pick them all up again. She walked back out and said to Levi, "I'll head down to join the others. Do you want me to bring you anything back?"

He gave her a gentle smile and said, "No, I'm fine. Thanks."

She took several steps, then turned to look at him. "Are

you going to take a break and sleep?"

"We all are. Two hours at a shot."

She nodded. "Then somebody should have woken me up an hour ago."

"Not going to happen. You were tired. You needed a little longer." He dropped his gaze to the paper in front of him.

She realized it wasn't so much that she'd been dismissed but that he was back on track with whatever project he was working on. She wandered down to the war room to find everybody in various states of discussion and planning. Bullard had stretched out on his big stretcher and was asleep, once again.

Brandon glanced at her and asked, "How do you feel?"

"Better, thanks," she admitted, smiling at Bullard's snoring. "But of course he doesn't sleep in a bedroom, does he?"

"I think he considers this his room," Brandon joked.

She glanced at him and said, "Did you get any rest?"

He grinned. "No, I've been making plans."

"So, it's your turn next?"

He glanced at his watch and said, "In about twenty-five minutes, yes."

Satisfied with that, she headed toward the kitchen. She nodded to Stone as he sat at the table, guarding the prisoners. The coffee was once again gone, so she put on another pot. The food was mostly gone and disarrayed. There was an odd muffin, a little bit of roast beef and some of the cheese still left and about half a loaf of bread. Hungry now after her nap, she made herself a roast beef sandwich, and, when the coffee was done, she took both back into the big central war room.

"Plans for what?" she asked, sitting down beside Brandon.

He looked at her and smiled. "You look like a two-year-old," he said gently. "There is still sleep in your eyes. You don't look like you are even here yet."

"I'm not," she said. "But I do feel better. Sorry for being so bitchy before. You were right to make me take a break."

"It's that argumentativeness that often tells us how bad off somebody is. The more you argue, the more you need to go," he said. "Don't forget we've all been there. We'll all be there again."

"Maybe not me," she said.

"So you're serious about getting out?"

"I don't know what I'm serious about. But I don't really want the killing on my front door anymore."

He smiled, reached over and gently rubbed her shoulders. "I don't blame you. It's not nice for any of us. But it's rare to have to kill someone. This scenario is an extreme case. Don't base your future on this."

She nodded. "In this location, chances are it'll always be a bit of the Wild West."

"Also in the US," he reminded her. "With one of the highest crime rates in the world, no city is completely free of it."

"I know. But I might be able to go a little longer between seeing dead people there. Plus I won't have all these men tied up in my kitchen who want to take over my home—or worse," she half joked. "Maybe it's having turned thirty that has me looking forward."

"Talk to Ice. I'm sure she's got a space for you at the compound."

"So she's said." She stared down at her plate. "I'm not sure yet." She took a bite of her sandwich and thought how much better it tasted when she wasn't exhausted. When she had polished it off, she took a sip of coffee.

He turned and, with a gaze of horror, exclaimed, "Is that fresh?"

She gave a fat smile and said, "Yes, I just made it."

He bolted to his feet and left at a fast-clipped pace toward the coffeepot. She chuckled.

A voice from the other side of her said softly, "Every time you get a chance, you go to Brandon."

She frowned and looked at her boss. "No, I don't."

"Yes, you do," he said with a gentle smile. "And that's the way it should be."

She shrugged. "I like him. But that doesn't mean anything."

"Sometimes our bodies and our instincts are way stronger and more intuitive than we give them credit for," he said, sitting up. "What you don't know is that, when you went to sleep, he sat outside your room to protect you while you were defenseless."

She froze in the act of lifting her coffee cup for a sip. She studied Bullard over the rim and said, "Really?"

When he nodded, something bloomed warm inside her. She didn't know when was the last time somebody had cared for her to that extent.

She slowly lowered the cup and said, "He would have done it for anyone. Besides, Ice was with me."

Bullard chuckled. "Yes, she was. Probably would have done it for any woman, quite true. He's that kind of guy. But he did it for you, and he did it first, before Levi even thought of it with Ice."

She wasn't sure what to make of that. It left her feeling a whole lot better about Brandon. She really did like him. It had been a long time since she had met anybody who attracted her. And Bullard was right. She gravitated to Brandon's side instinctively. Brandon returned before she had a chance to ask Bullard anything else.

Brandon sat down beside her and buried himself in his paperwork again until Bullard commented, "Did you tell her about the intruder you captured?"

Brandon shot Bullard a hard look and frowned. He shook his head. "No need to."

She turned to stare at him in amazement. "Where did you find him?"

He looked uncomfortable, then shifted slightly in his chair and refocused on the paperwork.

But she wasn't having any of it. She nudged his shoulder gently. "Where did you find him?"

He glared at her. "Approaching your bedroom."

She froze. "Oh, my God, he was on the same floor we were?"

Brandon gave a quick nod. "Yes."

"So there's another tunnel and stairway to each of the floors in this building?" Her gaze went from Bullard to Brandon and back to Bullard again.

"Yes," Bullard answered.

But Brandon was quick to add, "We've broadened our searches and discovered a couple more tunnels. But don't worry. We've booby-trapped them. That way we can use them, if needed, to escape the holding, but the gunrunners will suffer serious injury if barreling through any of them now."

She sank back in her chair, her gaze instinctively going to Bullard. He nodded and gave her a big smile. She glanced back at Brandon and whispered, "Thank you. For being there."

The stiffness went out of his back and shoulders, and she realized he thought she'd be angry at him—likely for being outside her room. Angry that he'd gone to watch over her. If she hadn't been quite so tired before going to lie down, she'd have realized they should be watching over each other. It was a smart thing to do. But he had realized what he needed to do, and he had done it regardless.

He gave her a small crooked smile and said, "You're welcome."

"I'm really not against help, you know."

"Good," he announced cheerfully. "Neither am I. It'll take all of us to protect that village."

"Protect that village?" She leaned forward to look at his plans. "Why are we protecting the village now?"

Brandon brought her up to speed on what they'd learned from the captured men.

She gasped. "No wonder they're fighting so hard to get in here." She looked to Bullard. "We can't just give them the guns, can we?"

He shook his head.

Brandon added, "Bullard's military friends are on the way too. Could be here in an hour or two."

"I'm all for protecting the innocent villagers. I might also be open to protecting the people who keep getting into my house because now I understand their motivation," Bullard said. "But I don't want to see a bloodbath once Konrad's military friends arrive."

"Is that likely to happen?"

"It depends on whether his friends are involved, doesn't it?"

BRANDON SPENT THE next twenty-five minutes trying to finalize his roughed-out plans. He wanted to hand them off to Levi and Bullard for their review and comments before Brandon took an hour to nap. He was scheduled for two, but he didn't think they'd have time. Plans needed to be set in motion and fast. If he didn't get this done, he wouldn't get the one hour either. He quickly finished off his map and notes. He stood and looked down at Kasha, saying, "I'll see you in a little bit."

She frowned, her gaze searching.

He smiled and said, "Just got to talk to Levi, and then I'm heading for my one hour."

"Have a good sleep."

He handed Levi his map and notes and said, "I'm early, but I'm gonna crash. We're short on time."

Levi nodded. "Go." He walked to where Bullard sat, drinking coffee.

Brandon watched the two put their heads together over his plan, and then he turned and headed to one of the rooms nearby. He didn't want to go upstairs, and there was plenty of space here. It wasn't exactly comfortable, but he just needed to crash and recharge.

In one room where they kept all the storage items, he'd seen some blankets. He pulled out a couple, went to the wall and lay down beneath the window. He closed his eyes, grateful for a moment to just be still. It seemed like only five minutes had passed when he woke up again. But, after checking his watch, he realized it was an hour and fifteen. He sat up, stretched, hating the grittiness of his eyes. His throat was dry, and his body was screaming for at least six more hours, but that wasn't going to happen.

Not right now. He got up and rubbed the sleep out of

his eyes. Instead of heading toward the group, he went to the washroom, wishing he could have a shower. That wasn't going to happen either.

He washed his face with cold water and gave it a good scrub. Slicking his hair back with his wet hands, he headed back out. As he stepped into the hallway, Kasha handed him a coffee. "It's the last one in the pot."

He gazed at it appreciatively. "Thank you so much."

"I've got another pot dripping." She smiled. "I'm not sure how quickly we're moving, but I figured coffee was never a bad idea."

Back in the war room, almost everyone was gathered. Levi looked up and smiled. "We're just going over the plan."

Brandon walked over and joined them. Although groggy, he needed to get his head in the game. "I figure we need to leave in fifteen minutes," Brandon said, looking at his watch.

Levi agreed. "It's going to come down, and it'll come down hard and fast."

"Well, let's hope we can save those who need saving and capture those who don't. The best plan is to have it all done before the military shows up."

"Agreed," Bullard said.

The next ten minutes was a scramble as everybody loaded up with weapons and piled into vehicles. Brandon hated to leave anybody at the holding, but they couldn't leave it unprotected. At the same time, they were thin on men on the ground. But, by utilizing as many as he could, they were spread out as watchdogs, all along the path. Two on either side of the village, so all four corners were covered; one on the road coming in; one on the road between the village and the holding; and two in the holding.

They left five minutes later—right on time. Bullard drove one vehicle and would drop off four men along the way and had already headed out. Brandon drove a second vehicle with the other two men. Kasha stayed behind to keep an eye on the prisoners, to run the command center and to keep the communication lines open. They had thought long and hard about bringing the captured men to help but decided they couldn't trust them yet. With their luck, the prisoners would shoot Bullard's team and take over everything as was their original plan.

Ice elected to stay behind too. She would be on the walkway and in constant contact with Kasha below.

Brandon knew it was too simple a plan. They were up against unknown numbers of men. They also didn't know if dupes were planted in the village. Did anybody even understand what the mercs were doing there in their town?

All the good guys weren't in position yet when the first alert came on their comms that three vehicles, loaded with men, were approaching the village from the far side. Brandon turned to the north and, in the distance, could see the sand cloud moving toward them. He frowned, then heard the confirmation that Levi and Stone were both at the entrance, hoping they'd be able to turn away the men. Given the speed those vehicles were going, no way that would happen.

Brandon was one of the first to enter the village. Bullard had arrived earlier to help communicate with the locals. The villagers were all currently hidden inside, away from the windows, hoping to avoid most of the oncoming war. Brandon's headset crackled, and Levi's voice filled it, saying, "The men are clearing a path with gunfire. We're hunkered down, taking cover."

Brandon frowned. "Talk about a waste of ammunition."

"No, they know we're there."

If they knew Levi's men and Bullard were here, had somebody from inside the holding told them? He tapped his comm to warn Kasha. "You and Ice be extra-alert. The men approaching the village seem to know we're here. So they must also know only two of you remain at the holding."

"How?"

"I don't know how," he said, "but you should be very wary of the prisoners."

"I'm sitting here in the kitchen, holding a rifle on them. One is sleeping, and the others are staring at me."

"Then I'd be worried about the one sleeping," he said. "Anything to throw you off."

"I'm on it."

"And don't speak in front of any of them. As soon as I sign off, leave the room to tell Ice. Expect another intruder."

"Yeah. Got it."

"Kasha …" He hesitated.

"What?"

"The smartest thing is to knock them all out." He clicked off his call. If he was there, he would do it. He wouldn't like it, but he'd do it because they couldn't take a chance on somebody else betraying them. One of their captives could be an outsider, and the villagers tied up with him would just be more collateral damage.

He knew Levi would have contacted Ice as well. She was alone on the walkway. That was enough to worry anybody.

Brandon could hear the gunfire before the vehicles arrived. He was tucked in behind one of the houses, looking for a way to take out the shooters. But, as soon as he fired, the attackers would return the gunfire in his direction. Yet that would also give Stone a better bead on the bad guys.

Brandon lined up his rifle and could see one of the men laughing as he fired aimlessly around the area. Brandon took aim and pulled the trigger. The man fell to the side, a hole in his forehead.

Brandon proceeded to take out two more shooters. A hail of bullets came his way, as expected, but he was already gone. He had three more targets picked out and moved swiftly from one to the other, firing but not wasting time or ammo.

Ammunition was too precious right now. Back at the holding, they had lots. They'd come away loaded for bear, but, at the rate the attackers were shooting, Levi's men and Bullard might not have enough. Brandon could hear Stone picking off others, based on the shouts, screams and more gunfire. Up ahead he saw Levi duck behind a small rise. The rise exploded with gunfire. Brandon counted sixteen men total on the three trucks, but that didn't mean there weren't more attackers coming on foot. Now fifteen on the trucks ...

Fourteen ...

As he watched, two more men fell from the truck, dead. The first truck rolled gently forward. Nobody was left alive to drive it. The second truck was trying to get out of the way and hide behind something. But there was no place for it to go. Brandon watched as the driver was killed at the entrance to the village. Those alive came out of the second vehicle and started firing as they raced toward the village. He took one out; Levi took another out. Realizing Stone would need more help as men raced in that direction, Brandon jumped across the main road, ran behind the second house and came up behind a shed in time to come face-to-face with another attacker. He pulled the trigger, and the man collapsed, a look of surprise on his face. Brandon kept moving. There was no time to waste and still at least eight gunmen to take down. Now that the intruders were able to hide among the villagers, it would be that much harder to find them and that much more dangerous to the villagers.

His headset crackled. "One bogey coming up behind you."

Brandon dropped, spun and fired. Down the bad guy went. "Thanks."

"No problem. We counted twenty-two men on three vehicles."

Brandon swore. "I only counted fifteen hits."

"I got eighteen marks down."

"Well, that's better odds." He moved swiftly through the village. He heard one shot. *Nineteen.* After that, an eerie silence filled the air. This was the dangerous point. Most of the enemy were down, and the ones left were angry and looking to survive. They were more dangerous now than ever. At the same time, the villagers would start thinking the worst was over, would let their guard down, and that made them targets. Once the gunmen held hostages, the whole game changed.

Brandon peered around the corner and caught sight of Stone who motioned to his right. Brandon slid back, came around the side and found a rebel on his belly inching forward.

Brandon's boot accidentally caught a stone that rolled forward. The gunman turned, raised his rifle and fired. But his body was already dancing midair as both Stone and Brandon nailed him.

"Twenty down," Brandon whispered to Levi.

The next half hour was tense, dusty and hot. The only way any of them were planning to go home was alive. They had two more men to take out. The worst was going to be if they accounted for twenty-one and couldn't find anybody else. Because, at that point, you wondered if you'd miscounted. That's when the last sucker had the advantage. He could either hide, run away or create chaos.

Another bullet shot past his head. Brandon dropped, rolled and came up behind the back of another building. He glanced around quickly. Hiding places were getting fewer and farther apart. Sitting still would always make him a target, so he picked up the pace and shifted around to where the vehicles were. What he didn't want was for any of the gunmen to take a vehicle and run. Levi's team and Bullard could use the vehicles themselves too. Sure enough, one of the gunmen was in Bullard's second vehicle, trying hard to get it started. Brandon came up behind him and whispered, "Hands up."

The gunman turned and had the rifle pointing at Brandon, midchest.

Brandon said, "Don't do it."

The gunman stared at him with a sly look and squeezed his finger. Brandon didn't have a choice. He fired. The gunman fell to the sand. He gasped, tried to say something and fell silent. In theory, there should only be one more left. "I've taken out one by the second truck," Brandon whispered.

"We're looking for one more."

Brandon knew it would come down to this. What he needed was a way to flush out the last guy. The man on the ground wore a helmet. He slipped it off and put it on his own head, then inserted the key and started the truck.

"I'm wearing the dead shooter's helmet. I'll see if I can flush out the last bad guy, letting him know there's a ride to take him home. Don't shoot me," he said.

He backed the truck up to the main road and moved quickly, his hand on the horn as he sped through the village. He checked on all sides to watch for any sign of the last gunman. Sure enough, a shot was fired in the air just up ahead to the right. He raced toward the man, motioning him to come. The man threw himself into the back of the truck, screaming something Brandon took to mean, "Go, go, go!"

Brandon did. But he spun around and raced back the way they came. The rest of his team was lined up at the end of the village. Brandon hit the brakes, and a dozen weapons were trained on the man in the back.

Brandon relaxed with a heavy sigh. "Are we done yet?" he asked Levi.

Levi smacked him on the shoulder and grinned. "I'd say we're done."

Bullard nodded. "Nice job."

Brandon laughed. It wasn't as fast or as simple as he'd wanted. But it did work, and that was all that counted. Up ahead he watched sand flying from more vehicles racing toward them. He pointed. "We've got company."

The men's faces turned grim. Brandon took the vehicle to the other end of the village and parked around the back of a house. He saw several women inside one of the homes clutching each other in terror. He held his finger up to his lips so they would know to stay quiet, and he crept around the corner.

The vehicles were military. They raced into the village and hit the brakes. One of the leaders started shouting. Nobody moved. Brandon watched as Bullard stepped forward and called out to him. The man took one look and grinned. "Bullard, what the hell, man? Did you kill everybody?"

Bullard, his rifle down but still at the ready, shook his head and said, "Just the gunrunners."

The officer raised his eyebrows. He laughed and said, "Good. In that case let's get you over to the holding so we can take possession of the weapons."

Bullard tilted his head to the side and said, "Who sent you?"

The man said something, but Brandon didn't understand.

Bullard shook his head. "Try again," he said.

The military officer straightened up, and anger crossed his face. Brandon realized what was going on. Bullard's contact may have sent these men, but that didn't mean these men had any intentions of following Konrad's orders.

Tucked in the house behind them, Levi had his phone in his hand. He was talking and taking photos. Bullard was trying to keep the officer talking as they figured out what was going on. Then finally Bullard nodded, pointed toward the holding and waited till the first vehicle passed.

At that point, Bullard and Levi ran for their wheels. Brandon wasn't sure what the hell was going on, but men were going everywhere. He got back into his truck and drove around to where Levi loaded up his men in the other truck with Bullard. When Levi jumped in the truck with Brandon, he asked Levi, "What the hell's going on?"

"This is the team supposedly sent by Konrad, Bullard's contact," Levi said. He turned and gave Brandon a hard glare. "While Bullard trusts Konrad, he doesn't trust any of these guys. Ice knows they're coming. We've also got a phone call in to Konrad. I highly suspect these guys will take the weapons and run."

"Do we stop them?"

Levi snorted. "Welcome to the law in this country. That's a decision we may not get a choice about."

Brandon turned on the engine again and headed toward home. Kasha was there with the prisoners. No way in hell he wanted her to meet this lot alone.

Chapter 11

KASHA HADN'T HAD any contact with Levi's men or Bullard in over thirty minutes, and it was killing her. She wanted an update. When her phone rang, it was Ice, and the message she shared wasn't what Kasha wanted to hear. "How many military are coming?"

"Two vehicles. Bullard's contact says those men are his."

"Do we trust them?"

"I'm not sure it's a matter of trusting them as much as making sure somebody is keeping an eye on them."

"So is his contact on his way?"

"He is. He's due to land in about twenty minutes at the airstrip."

"Okay, that's good. Then it's his responsibility if they take the weapons. If these guys steal them, then at least he can track them."

"Exactly," Ice said, her voice changing. "You need to be very careful right now. What about the bodies?"

"No idea. Hopefully the military will take them away."

"That would be good."

Kasha frowned. She hoped it was over. It had been quiet at the holding, but that didn't mean it would stay quiet. She put on coffee, keeping her weapon trained on the five prisoners the whole time.

She understood Brandon's suggestion about knocking

them out, but, as she talked to the men, she tried hard to explain what her people were doing and why.

One man seemed relieved. He had a wife and a baby in the village. Another just stared at her, and a third one, the one supposedly sleeping, had woken up. He snorted and closed his eyes. She figured he would be trouble no matter what. The remaining pair were too scared to speak or didn't understand English or her dialect of Arabic. With the coffee made, she picked up the weapon and turned back to the men, only to find one standing, his ties loose on the ground. It was the one who'd been sleeping.

She pointed the rifle at him, and he laughed. He let rip a stream of invectives about how women shouldn't carry weapons and how she wasn't strong enough. Women should have babies and look after their men, according to him. A common theme throughout many third-world countries. But it had never been her thing.

She told him, "Don't move, or I *will* shoot."

He spat on the floor and walked toward her. She raised the rifle and knew he would push it. Rather than deal with killing another person, she lowered the weapon to point it at his groin. He stopped, and anger such as she hadn't seen in a long time ripped through his face. But she stood steady. She could hear the vehicles coming toward her. The man looked in the direction of the garage and said something she didn't quite understand.

"Go sit down," she said, "or I will turn you into an eunuch."

He glared at her, hate dripping from his very pores. She shuddered but couldn't ignore it. Neither could she turn her back on him. If she got too close, she knew he would be all over her. She should have knocked him out. She debated her options and realized that really there was only one option. Just as she made her decision, he spun and kicked. She fired. His knee went out from under him as the bullet passed through the joint. He shouted, grasping at his leg.

She didn't move. In a hard voice she said, "Get your ass back over to your friends."

Slowly, sobbing in pain, he shifted until he was lying on the floor beside the other four men. She glanced at them, and, instead of anger in their gazes, there was relief. She realized that if anybody here didn't deserve a chance, it was the one she'd shot. The other men were happy to see him taken out of the picture. She motioned toward the bleeding man. "Is he one of the betraying assholes?"

The man with the wife and child, who talked freely, nodded. "He made us help them. He's part of the group who was happy to raze the village." He glared at the man on the floor. "You should shoot him again and this time kill him."

The man on the ground sobbed.

She turned to look at one of the men who'd been silent. "What do you say about him?" The man looked up, and there was hate in his eyes, but it wasn't directed at her. "He killed my brother. And he shot the men forced to stand guard outside the holding. They were innocent villagers."

"Your brother?"

"My brother's the one who was forced to kill all the injured men. They had his wife and sons. They said, if he didn't kill all the survivors, they would shoot him. But then, when he made it to the airstrip, they shot him anyway." He turned, spat at the man on the ground and said, "He shot my brother. Then he shot my brother's wife too."

She stared at the man on the ground. He'd stopped crying, but now just sheer anger and hatred and, yes, fear was in his eyes. "I should shoot you. It would be good for you to die at a woman's hand," she snapped. "But I'd rather see you rot in a jail with no food and no water for days on end."

The jails here were notorious. The death toll was high from poor food, unsanitary conditions and fights among the men. She didn't know much about the judicial system, but it would probably be a whole lot nicer of her to shoot him now than to force him through that. The thing was, she didn't feel like being nice. He was an asshole. He deserved everything coming to him.

In the distance, she heard vehicles coming closer. She cast a hard look at the prisoners and walked to the window for a better look.

Two military vehicles came to a dust-raising stop, one in front of the underground garage entrance and the other probably headed outside the locked front gate. Two men hopped out of the first vehicle, grabbed their weapons and took a stance on either side of the garage door entrance. She frowned, tapped her comm. "Ice, I'm not liking this," she said.

"Explain."

She quickly told Ice where the military men were.

"Three more vehicles are coming—one from the airstrip, two from town," Ice said. "Two of our guys should be driving the two trucks from the village. Bullard's military contact should be the one arriving from the airstrip. However, we can't trust anybody until we see the men. So don't let anybody in."

Kasha had to admit that had been her thought too. The local military, who she didn't trust, could wait until the rest of the men arrived. "Can you see where the other vehicle went?"

"It's coming around the front here. It's looking for an entrance at the front gate." Then her voice dropped. "Oops," she said. "They have just climbed over the gates."

"Dammit, Bullard was supposed to get that set up. But we didn't have time."

"What was he planning on?" Ice's voice was breathless, as if running.

Kasha could just imagine Ice moving quickly around the rooftop, trying to get in position to keep an eye on the men who were already jumping over the gate. "He was going to electrify it. Put underground sensors and alarms in the house."

"Right. Yeah, he needs to get on that. The men are twenty feet from the front door."

"Chances are it's not locked," Kasha said.

Ice chuckled. "Men like this, they won't give a shit if it's locked or not. Expect gunfire as they blast their way through."

"I thought this was the military?"

"It is. At least they're wearing military uniforms. Beyond that we can't count on anything," Ice's voice deepened. "How are you set for ammo?"

"I've only shot one man," Kasha said drily. "So I'm still fine."

Ice paused, as if startled. She asked, "Did you kill him?"

"No. I blew his knee apart."

"Good. If he makes a move, this time kill him. These men are dangerous."

On that note, Kasha turned to study the men, but nothing had changed. The one on the ground was still moaning, and the other four were sitting quietly, but their eyes were wide and alert. They knew something was going down. Just then, she heard gunfire. The captives' eyes took on a shocked look, and they started to yell at her. She held her finger to her lips. "It's the military, but I don't know if it's the good military or the bad military."

From the look in their eyes, they understood. So she said in a warning note, "I highly suggest you stay quiet until we know more. If you give me any reason, ... *any* reason," she repeated for emphasis, "I'll kill you myself."

With a hard glance, she walked to the monitors, laid down the rifle and clicked on the keys. A ton of potential lay in this holding, but it would take a lot of electronics to set it up properly. Right now, these new guys would be able to come through the house at whatever pace they wanted. But, if they didn't know the layout, they wouldn't find their way to the cache in the garage very quickly or to her in the kitchen or Ice on the rooftop.

However, if they knew the layout, she could expect company any second. She checked the cameras here on the first floor. They weren't even wall-mounted yet. They were just stuck in corners at the main entrances. She caught sight of two men, both with their weapons ready, as if looking for an attack. She watched as they immediately came toward her. With her heart sinking and her chest seizing, she realized they were coming directly here. She couldn't use the comm without letting the men in the room know what she'd seen. They said they didn't speak English, but they could still understand more than they let on. She didn't want to give them any more information than she had to. And she'd probably already said too much.

She tapped on her headpiece in Morse code.

Ice answered in code. She was on her way down. Her instructions were simple to follow because Kasha had already done it. She was told to hide. She was already tucked inside one of the multiple pantry cabinets. She knew the arriving military would see the captives, and that would start something. Almost as soon as she had the thought, she heard footsteps running in, then a sudden silence, followed by sharp orders. Two of the villagers tried to explain.

The man on the floor told them where she hid.

She lifted her rifle, stepped out and said, "Hands up."

BRANDON COULD SEE the holding up ahead. He could also see one military vehicle parked outside the gate and another in front of the underground garage entrance. He hoped all was well, but his gut said it wasn't. They had already heard from Ice that two men had jumped the gate in front. Either they suspected terrorists were inside or they were planning on taking out the place. Neither was a good scenario. Brandon parked his vehicle outside the garage just as Levi hopped out and swept down toward the garage. But it was still locked from the inside. Levi spoke to Ice, asking if she could open it. Her response was an immediate "*No.*"

They looked for another entrance but couldn't find one. They weren't far from the tunnel though. With the same thought, they raced toward it. At the entrance, one crouched low and one stood high as they did a sweep to make sure it was empty. As soon as they entered, Levi told Ice where they were. Brandon knew things had gone from bad to worse, but they were here now.

When they finally crept up the stairs and reached the kitchen pantry, they could hear yelling. Brandon went ahead and slipped to the left, while Levi went right. Brandon wasn't exactly sure who was in the kitchen as most of the language was foreign.

Then he heard Kasha's voice, cold and hard. He didn't understand a word she said, but he understood the meaning.

He snuck farther along the wall, peering through the cracks in the pantry doorways, looking for more intruders. How many men had entered? From where he stood, the five captives were accounted for: one on the kitchen floor amid his blood plus four still tied to chairs. He could see Kasha holding a rifle on two new arrivals, both standing, both in military uniforms. Both their backs were to him.

With a hand motion to Levi, he swept past and around the two newcomers so fast that both the uniformed men turned to see who was coming up behind them and now they had a standoff. The military men barked orders, but Brandon and Levi ignored them. Kasha snapped something back at the men. They turned and glared at her.

She shrugged. "They don't want to lower their weapons," she said. "They say they are military police, and we are to drop our weapons."

"That's nice," Brandon said. "They came into Bullard's house without warning, jumped over the gate and broke down the doors. They have no reason to interfere."

At Bullard's name, she frowned. "How is he?"

Levi chuckled. "Bullard's fine. He's on his way."

She nodded.

The military men slowly lowered their weapons. Levi motioned for them to step apart, and then he disarmed them. Without weapons, the men were ushered toward the other prisoners and told to sit down. Kasha walked toward Brandon. Instinctively he opened his arms and tugged her in for a hug.

She squeezed him back, and he held her for a long moment. Then he said, "What did they have to say?"

She pointed at the man on the ground. "He told the military police where I was hiding."

Brandon turned his attention to the bloodied man. "You shot him?"

"Yeah, I did. I should've killed him," she snapped. "The others are from the village. One has a wife and a daughter. He was forced into helping, and he would do anything to save his family. Another has a similar story. Two have remained mostly silent, but one finally spoke up. His brother was the shooter from the last night who then was killed. But the one on the floor with my bullet in his knee is just an asshole. He was part of the group who forced the village men into this." She turned to look at Brandon. "What about the village?"

"Secure. As far as we can see, everybody is fine there."

"What about those coming from the airstrip?"

"That's Bullard's military contact."

Brandon walked over to the man with the bullet hole in his knee. He kicked it hard. The man screamed. He said to Kasha, "You tell him that's for him throwing you to the wolves."

She snorted. "Doesn't matter. He's a traitor to everybody. Whoever pays him the most is who he looks after."

Brandon looked at the other prisoners. "Are you sure these men didn't say anything to the police?"

She shook her head. "No, they didn't say anything."

The two men she'd conversed with the most looked nervously from one to the other, and the father spoke up. Kasha answered him. She turned to Brandon and said, "He says he didn't do anything wrong. He'd like to make it up to the new owner. He didn't want to get involved, but he had no choice."

Brandon nodded and eased back slightly. As soon as the four villagers saw that, they settled into their chairs. They weren't going anywhere, tied up as they were. As for the asshole on the ground, Brandon said, "You should have killed him."

He heard Levi's headset squawk, and Levi motioned toward the front door. Leaning closer to Kasha, Brandon whispered, "More company. I'm heading there."

She took a better position so she had a good aim on everyone.

Brandon grinned. A girl after his own heart. He ran out the kitchen and down the hall to open the front door. The front gate was still locked. But this time Bullard was in the vehicle. Brandon raced to the gate and opened it. After letting Bullard and the rest of Levi's team in, the two men greeted each other. "We've got two military men in the kitchen, another two were standing guard by the garage, plus the five captives. Everyone else is fine."

Bullard nodded. He motioned behind him to another jeep, this one carrying four military men. "I know these four," Bullard said.

"Do you think they are on the same side as the other soldiers inside?" Brandon asked.

"No." Bullard smiled. "But we should have a talk with those two you have in the kitchen."

"You may have better luck with the two outside the garage," Ice yelled from the rooftop.

"Why?" Brandon hollered.

"I left them alive to get answers from, but they'll need Bullard's medical expertise," Ice's voice came again.

Bullard slapped Brandon on the shoulder. "Too bad

she's taken, boy. Of course, Kasha is still available."

Brandon shook his head. "Kasha would have your head for saying that."

"She would indeed. See? You already understand her."

The jeep rolled to a stop as the men approached, and Brandon shut the gate behind the military vehicle. He watched as Bullard's contact got out, waiting for Bullard to walk over. After greeting the men, Bullard led the way into the house and to the central war room area. There, introductions were made. Within minutes they led the new arrivals to the kitchen where the men were being held. Kasha stepped back, still holding her weapon on the men.

The man Bullard appeared to trust the most, Konrad, stepped forward and barked something out in a language Brandon didn't understand to the two other military police. They pulled out their identifications and handed them over. Konrad looked at them carefully. He picked up his phone and walked to another part of the room, so he could have his phone call in private. Brandon and Levi exchanged raised eyebrows. Brandon said, "We need to clean up the garbage outside the garage doors. Ice apparently injured two."

"I'm coming with you," Kasha said. She handed her weapon to Levi. "Let's bring a stretcher."

She pulled out a large stretcher from one of the pantry cabinets. Brandon looked at it and said, "I'm still surprised there would be such a thing here. And why so many?"

"Bullard brought several with him." Kasha laughed. "Says he never travels anywhere without at least two of them."

Levi snorted. "He came to us several times without them."

Bullard's loud voice boomed through the room. "That's

because I knew Ice already had them. You never know when you will need a gurney." He pointed at the one Kasha was setting up on its wheels and said, "Look. Right now we need two of them." He twisted to look at the asshole on the ground. "I don't know what to do with that one."

Konrad snapped, "He's coming with me."

Brandon stopped. "Why?"

Konrad growled, "He's on our Most Wanted list."

"What about these two soldiers?"

He spat on the ground. "They will be court-martialed for their activities."

The two men looked at each other nervously.

Kasha stepped up beside Brandon and asked, "And the two men we have outside?"

Konrad nodded. "They will be coming with us too."

"You need a bigger plane," Bullard said. "We have two more dead in a freezer area."

Konrad sighed. "We need a lot of things. But first and foremost, we need loyal men." He shot a disgusted look at his officers. "These two are not good examples."

"What did they have to do with this?"

"According to our intel, these two uniforms and the two from outside are most likely friends with the men you shot attacking the village and set up this place for the gunrunning."

"Well then, why the hell did they not know it was for sale, and why didn't they buy it?"

"It's been for sale for a long time. They just helped themselves and lived here regardless. They figured, if it was ever sold, they could chase away the new owners."

Bullard walked closer to the man on the ground who cringed and tried to shift backward. Brandon listened as

Bullard ripped into him in the same language Kasha had used and then turned his attention to the two military guys. Before he was done, they were all desperate to get away.

Kasha on the other hand grinned like a two-year-old. "It does my heart good to hear Bullard open up like that," she whispered, leaning into Brandon.

"I'm just sorry I didn't understand a word of it," Brandon admitted. "It sounded lovely though."

She chuckled. "It was." She straightened, grabbed the gurney and said, "Come on. Let's get the other men. When the military leaves, they can take everyone. Dead or alive."

Levi called back, "We also have to load up the weapons. Konrad's taking them back with him. With the serial numbers, they should be able to trace where they were manufactured and hopefully find the middlemen."

Brandon nodded. With Kasha at his side, he led the way to the garage. As soon as they opened it, the two men were visible beside their military vehicle. Kasha took one look and whistled. "Ice does good work."

Both men were down, both legs badly damaged. But they'd live. And most likely they'd talk. That would save their lives more than anything would. They loaded both men on one gurney and slowly pushed them back toward the crowd in the central war room.

When the two military men from the kitchen saw the other two military policemen, they started yelling at the top of their lungs. Brandon had been in a lot of countries in the world, and he had heard a lot of languages, but, in this last couple hours, he wished he understood this language more than any other. He looked to Kasha for a translation.

"They say they were forced to help." She shrugged. "It's the same old story of betrayal. Same thing everywhere, no matter what language they speak."

The next hour was chaotic. Apparently Konrad had arrived in a bigger plane than expected, but it still wasn't big enough for the cache of weapons plus all the prisoners and the dead bodies involved and Konrad and his three men. With a second plane on its way for Konrad and the weapons cache, the real military took the injured prisoners, the fake military guys and the dead. Under a fully armed escort, the prisoners most likely spilled their guts before they even made it to the landing spot.

Brandon didn't know much about the medical system here, except that it was expensive and nonexistent in many places. But at least the injured were still alive. Brandon could make peace with whatever happened to them later.

All in all, Brandon would say this was a good day's work, and it wasn't yet 3:00 p.m.

Chapter 12

EVERYTHING ELSE WAS almost anticlimactic now. Kasha watched from the background as the men were removed first, to board the plane standing by. The second plane must have arrived shortly thereafter as more military men soon began moving the weaponry. They were even taking the dog. Apparently, Brandon had been checking on it since he'd arrived, making sure it had food and water.

Another factor in his favor. She manned the coffeepot and pulled out the last of the food. Might as well have everybody eat it all up before they left. According to Bullard, they wouldn't be staying long. She was ready to leave. He wanted to pull out in a couple hours. She doubted they'd make it by then. So she was surprised when Bullard turned to her an hour later and asked, "Are you packed and ready to go?"

She crossed her arms over her chest and said, "I was ready a long time ago."

He gave her an understanding look. "Not exactly the quick trip to check out the place, was it?"

"No. Of course the military didn't take all the weapons. They took the corpses, and they took all the prisoners, and they took a lot of the weapons," she said with a stern look. "But you didn't hand everything over. Why?"

He raised his eyebrows. "I handed most of it over. Remember when I purchased the private property and signed all the documents?"

She nodded. "I do."

"It came *as is*. Meaning all contents were mine."

She shook her head. "That logic might work in a Western world. It doesn't wash here."

"I figured some of it was payment for all the shit that just went down, not to mention I handed over the traitors within their own ranks, a lot of weapons that probably they'd already seized once. Now at least with the serial numbers they should be able to track down what happened here. If we're lucky, we might have a better relationship with the villagers now."

"That's another thing. You let them take the four men from the village."

He gave her a gentle smile. "Did I?"

She frowned. "Didn't you?"

He shook his head. "Part of the negotiation was those four would go back to the village. Of course they owe me now," he said with an annoying smile. "I hope they remember that."

She rolled her eyes. "So, what you're saying is, you now have four devoted slaves."

He gave her a fat grin. "Yep. Life can't be all bad if I've got that."

"The villagers are poor. They need work."

"We'll look at that—not today, not tomorrow, but down the road. In the meantime, this place needs to be packed up, the rest of the weapons secured, and we must have men in place at all times."

"Have we got the right men for the job?"

He pursed his lips and got a faraway look in his eyes.

"I'll send a couple to manage the place along with a few tradesmen. We might as well get more of the renovations done. Could hire some locals to help out too."

"Can you trust them?" she asked in a dry tone.

Again that fat grin slid out. "I do learn from my mistakes. It might take me a little while, but eventually I learn. The villagers did me wrong. Hopefully we're at square one again. But I won't make the same mistake twice."

"How can you secure all of this then?"

"First off, they won't know what's here because, as far as they're concerned, the military took all the weapons with them. Second, we're setting up cameras. I'm bringing in a crew right away to do that. We'll patch that feed into our center at the estate. And third, we'll rig this place with traps. If anybody goes after anything, it'll set off a chain of events they're going to regret."

She nodded. "That's fair. So are you ready to go now?"

"I hope so." Bullard nodded. "And we now have a second holding. We have a village prepared to at least make some peace with us. We came out okay in terms of weapons. Which are here now, so I don't have to transport new ones, and this is really a beautiful place."

She nodded. "It is. But it's not a place I want to be."

"You're still looking to move?" Bullard smiled at her. "Brandon is based in the US."

"Yes, I am still thinking about it," she said. "And not because of Brandon."

"Keep protesting," he teased. "Maybe someone will believe you."

She rolled her eyes at him. She grabbed the bags and boxes they had packed and made one trip to the vehicle. There she ran into Brandon and engaged his help to load the rest into the vehicles. Bullard's team would arrive at this holding in the morning, and several of the guys here now would be staying behind to make the transfer smoother. They needed to have an onsite meeting to go over the tunnels and a few other issues about the place. She knew Bullard would get the electronics set up as fast as he could. That would mean a team of specialists coming in.

He might do the work himself. He was fussy, and that was right up his alley. Besides, this was his place. He would want this one secure. For herself, she was just happy to leave. She'd been with Bullard for five years, and making the move back to the US was huge. But it felt like time.

When she finally got onto the airplane and buckled up, it seemed she'd been traveling since forever. Brandon sat down beside her and squeezed her hand. She stared at their entwined fingers. She wasn't sure how they had come to this. She liked him, admired him, respected him, and that was a hell of a lot to go on. But how much of a future could they possibly have? She didn't even know where she would land in the States. The fact that he worked for Ice meant they could still possibly see each other. It felt odd. But then her whole world felt odd right now. She smiled at him and said, "Not quite the trip you envisioned, right?"

"Definitely not. But I'm adaptable," he said with a smile.

"How long have you worked for Levi and Ice?"

"Just a few days before I came here. Several of my friends work for them. It seemed like a natural step."

"A lot of Bullard's men say the same thing. When you leave the military, you have all these skills you can't use anymore. Those jobs fill a need in many ways."

"On both sides. Not everybody in the world has access to military assistance. Therefore, people like us fill that void as well."

The others found a seat and dropped their luggage and gear nearby. When everybody was finally seated, the pilot moved forward to the cockpit. They were airborne ten minutes later. It was a long flight. She'd like to come back in a year or two and see what Bullard had done with the place but was happy to leave it for now.

"I guess it's back to the US for you?" she asked.

He squeezed her fingers, leaned his head back and closed his eyes. "Yes. It will be." He rolled his head toward her and opened his eyes. "Come with me."

She froze like a deer caught in headlights.

"It would be a good chance for you to see how Levi and Ice's outfit runs. Meet the rest of the guys and see if it's something you want to be part of."

She realized he was asking her to come for a visit. As a friend. She sagged back in her chair, confused and slightly disoriented. How was it she'd been disappointed at that realization? She hadn't known him for long. But their circumstances had been intense. She shook her head. "I hadn't planned on leaving right now."

He thought about that for a moment. "Bullard was talking about sending somebody over for Ice as it is."

"For what?"

"New testing on their security system. Looking at upgrades."

"Well, he won't be sending me," she said. "I don't know anything about security."

"Maybe not but you showed damn fine form when we were attacked."

She chuckled. "You mean, because I can hold a weapon, knock down bad guys and handle myself under fire?"

His grin widened. "Absolutely. Perfect wifely qualities." He chuckled at his own words.

She stared. "That's not normally something people would laugh about."

"Sure it is. Lots of guys think the only thing a woman needs to do is make a sandwich."

She frowned at him and said, "But that's all I did make."

He nodded his head, still chuckling. "Don't worry about it. It's just a joke. The thing is, what you did was adapt. Circumstances changed. They went from bad to terrible and then to good and down to horrible again. Each time you handled yourself well."

"If you're looking for another sandwich, I don't have anything to give you," she said drily.

"Not used to getting compliments, are you?"

She wanted to drop her gaze from the intensity in his. But he wasn't having anything to do with it. She wondered if anybody else was watching them. Surely they must be. Yet there was an intimate feel to their conversation. It made her uncomfortable. As if understanding that, he rolled his head back and closed his eyes. "Wake me before we land."

And just like that, he fell asleep. She watched him. She wished she could fall asleep at will. She settled into her chair and waited. Bullard was across the aisle, talking to Levi. He caught her gaze and motioned at her hand. She glanced down to see her fingers still entwined with Brandon's. She frowned at them. Such an odd thing. Should she pull her hand away? She glanced back at Bullard to find him grinning with an approving look. She shook her head and tried to disengage her fingers, but Brandon—whether asleep or not—clamped down his fingers and held hers firmly.

With a wince she sighed, hating that now Levi and Stone

were looking at her with the same look. She glared at them all.

They grinned back at her. She didn't know what Bullard would say if she asked for time to spend with Brandon and Levi's crew at the compound. It was a good idea. Maybe when she got there, she wouldn't like it. She would miss Bullard terribly too.

Still, one didn't stay at a job just because you liked your boss. The trouble was, she wasn't even sure what work she wanted to do. With Bullard, she had been everything from a bodyguard to a personal assistant. That was hardly something Ice and Levi needed. Kasha had other skills, but she hadn't really thought about marketing them. As they approached Bullard's huge home estate, she wondered why she was even looking at leaving. It was beautiful here.

Only she'd been thinking about going home for a long time. The plane started its descent. She squeezed Brandon's fingers, and his eyes flew open.

Although his gaze was slightly unfocused, it didn't take him long to return to sharp awareness. "Are we almost there?"

She pointed in the distance.

He leaned over so he could look out the window. "Good enough. Hope he's got food at home."

She chuckled. "Is that all you guys think about?"

He shot her a look that was more intimate than she expected, and he whispered, "Absolutely not."

Her cheeks flushed red, and she turned away, gathering her thoughts. With just a few comments, this man could send her temperature flying.

She could walk through wars, take on attackers and intruders, but he only had to say a couple nice comments, and she fell to pieces. He might be good at a lot of things, but he was devastating when it came to women. She sighed. "You probably have lots of relationships, don't you?"

He was startled, then leaned over and in a low voice said, "I've had several, yes, but always one at a time."

She studied her fingers still held in Brandon's grip. At least that was one thing. She didn't think she could handle a man who didn't know how to be monogamous. A lot of things in life she could tolerate, but a cheating partner was not one of them. Just then the pilot's voice came over the loudspeaker. With their seat belts buckled, they waited to land. It was smooth, but then the pilot who worked for Bullard had had lots of practice. When they finally disembarked, several vehicles drove toward them. She hopped into the front of the first one and threw her arms around Dave.

He gave her a hug right back. "You've had an exciting time, I hear."

She snorted. "Well, I don't know who you'd have heard that from. In truth, it was an incredibly odd time with lots of action and lots of excitement. You know, the usual death, blood, gore and of course survival."

"Maybe that's not a bad thing," Dave said.

"Maybe that's not a good thing either," she said.

He patted her knee. "You're home, safe and sound. That's what counts."

She smiled and settled in. Brandon was in the back seat with Harrison and Stone. The others had gotten into the vehicles behind her. She was happy to be home. She just didn't know if she was meant to stay. Dave took them directly to the estate, wasted no time on a sightseeing tour. Then again the trip was only a few minutes. The sun was still out, and all she wanted was a hot shower and some food and a dip in the pool. "The guys are hungry," she said to Dave.

"Of course they are. Not to worry. I've got it taken care of."

She smiled. "Good, I was shitty at cooking duties."

Brandon leaned forward and said, "But she makes a mean sandwich."

Dave smirked. "She can cook."

"Don't go telling him that," she cried. "I'll always be dumped on kitchen duty then."

Behind them Harrison asked, "Food? Any chance of a meal, Dave?"

Dave gave a hefty laugh. "Indeed, there is. It's waiting for us." He twisted slightly, gave Harrison a good look and said, "Not to mention cold beers."

In the rearview mirror, she watched Stone's face light up like a candelabrum. She realized it wasn't just her who had suffered—all the men had had a rough few days. "I'm getting changed and going straight into the pool."

"I saw the pool, but I never did get a chance to take a close look at it," Brandon said.

"You should. It's beautiful. Bullard designed the back-yard himself and did a lot of the work too," Dave added.

As soon as they pulled in, she hopped out, grabbed her bag, picked up one of the boxes and rushed inside. She carried on right through to the kitchen where she dropped the box. It was the leftover foodstuffs. Not that there was much. With a glance at the pool, twinkling so beautifully in the sunshine, she said, "I'll be back in five."

She strode down the hall and up the stairs. In her room she dropped her bag and, rummaging in her dresser, found a bathing suit. She changed, grabbed a cover-up and a towel, slipped her feet into thongs and headed back downstairs. She bypassed the kitchen and anywhere there appeared to be people. She just wanted to be alone. Outside she tossed her cover-up, dropped her towel and, walking around to the deep end, dove in. As soon as the water closed over her head, she could feel her stress melting away. God, she loved water; she loved swimming.

She rolled, flipped, came to the surface and then struck out strongly for the other end of the pool. This was exactly what she needed. She lost count of the number of times she went from end to end. Letting her body set the rhythm, her mind replayed all they'd been through. If she didn't, the experiences would lock up inside, and she wouldn't move forward.

BRANDON STILL STOOD in the kitchen when he saw Kasha come down the stairs and head outside. He twisted so he could look out the window as she approached the pool. Seeing her in a tiny bikini, his eyebrows went straight up. Tall, lean, small-breasted, with legs that went on forever. She was damn perfect. She walked around to the deep end, completely unconscious of her beauty. She took a breath and dove in—a perfectly clean, crisp dive—and then proceeded to swim. She was obviously comfortable in the water and made good use of the pool.

Bullard smacked him on the shoulder and said, "What are you waiting for?"

Brandon shot him a sideways look and said, "You got any trunks for me?"

Bullard pointed to the small cabana on the other side of the pool. "That's the changing room. It's fully stocked. Go find something your size and get in."

Nobody had to tell him twice. He was hot, tired and cranky. But seeing the mermaid, wow, talk about a mood changer. He walked away from the main house and headed toward the small cabana. When he stepped inside, he realized everything was sized from small to large on labeled shelves. He pulled on a pair of shorts that looked to be about right. They were a little loose but had a drawstring. Folding his clothes, he put them on one of the shelves and stepped outside.

Kasha was still doing laps. He walked to the diving board, took a couple experimental bounces and did a clean dive off the end. It had been a long time since he had any inclination to fool around in a pool. This was fun.

He'd been a SEAL. For him that said everything. There was a lot of tension and leftover fatigue from what they'd been through. A good workout would make him feel better. He fell into a rhythm beside her. She hadn't acknowledged his presence in any way, but he knew she had to have known he arrived.

Or at least that somebody had joined her. With the two of them keeping abreast of each other, they moved strongly through the pool, lap after lap after lap. Finally he wondered if she would ever tire because he was already feeling it in his muscles. He hadn't swum like this in weeks. He hated to think he was getting out of shape, but it wasn't so much that as dealing with unfamiliar movements.

Muscles that hadn't been worked in a while needed to be worked again. Levi and Ice had talked about putting in a pool, and he knew it was in the works, but he didn't know when the plan was set to start. A pool in Texas would be ideal. If they did it right, maybe with solar panels and proper heaters, they could run that pool most of the year. He'd have to mention it to them when they got back to the compound.

The pool was also a big expenditure, but exercise was important, and he loved swimming, so loved the idea of having those plans move forward. Ice herself was a strong swimmer. She had bemoaned the fact many times that there was no place for her to have a good swim without driving forty-five minutes into town.

Sure, she had a lot of hand-to-hand combat workouts, and the weight gym and all the fitness equipment they needed were available at the compound, but, as Brandon was finding out, those used a different set of muscles than swimming. Finally he realized Kasha had slowed and came to a stop at one end. He pulled up beside her, crossed his arms and rested against the pool's edge. He glanced over at her and said, "You're a strong swimmer."

She flashed him a smile. "I used to be a competitive swimmer in school."

"That explains it," he said. "I wasn't sure I'd be able to keep up," he admitted.

She laughed. "No worries there. I was starting to run out of steam a while ago. I figured, if I could get myself exhausted enough, I wouldn't keep having the last forty-eight hours on an endless loop in my mind instead of sleeping tonight."

"None of us got much in the way of sleep the last couple nights."

"No. We'll probably all need to crash early tonight. Food first though." She looked around to see Dave standing at the other end. "Is dinner ready, Dave?"

He nodded. "We're going to eat outside, so maybe just throw your cover-up on and come and join us at the table."

She nodded. They walked out at the shallow end, and she picked up a towel. He hadn't even thought of a towel.

She pointed at the cabana and said, "There's a whole stack of them over there."

He pulled out a towel and dried off. In a low voice he said, "Do I need a shirt to show up for a meal?"

She laughed and said, "No, but you can throw on your T-shirt if you want." She threw her cover-up over her head. It hid most of her bikini and bare skin, but it enticed with the peekaboo holes that showed just enough to tantalize and tease.

He donned his T-shirt and walked barefoot with her to the table. He stopped for a moment and just stared. The others were looking at him, big fat grins on their faces.

"It's only because Dave is a really nice guy that he called you to eat with us," Stone said. He nodded toward the laden table. "Otherwise, I would have waited 'til I was done."

Brandon chuckled. "Not even you can eat all the food here," he said, grabbing an empty chair.

Stone said, "Maybe not, but I would have given it a good try. Besides, I know Dave. There'll be dessert after all this too."

Brandon stared at the tableful of roast beef and roast chicken salads and cooked vegetables and potatoes, then turned his head to Stone. "Dessert?" he asked with hope.

Stone nodded. "Dave always bakes."

The laughter slowed down as everyone filled their plates and started to eat. For ten minutes there were just the sounds of happy people munching away.

Brandon didn't really want to fill up too much on this course if dessert was coming, but, once his stomach realized real food was in the offing, he couldn't get full.

Dave sat benignly at one end with a big fatherly smile on his face. Bullard had showed up and sat at the other.

Brandon noticed the fatigue pulling at him, but then they all looked the same. He felt much better mentally after his swim in the pool, but the physical tiredness remained inside. It was what happened when you went too long without adequate sleep. It was hard to focus on anything.

When Bullard was done, he pushed his plate back with the happy sigh. "Damn, it's good to be home."

"Then why is it we left?" Kasha asked with a smile.

Bullard laughed. "I thought it would be a good idea to have a second holding somewhere."

Levi piped up, "How do you feel about it now?"

Bullard's face sobered. "That's a good question. It'll take a lot of money to bring the second holding up to snuff. I could turn around and sell it, but I'm not sure I would get anything for it right now."

"You got it cheap as it is," Ice said. "Think about it. Don't make a hasty decision either way."

Bullard nodded. "If nothing else, it's a home away from home. A place to go when we need to get away or when we need a refuge."

"You've already got several of those," Kasha said.

"Sure, but none around here. I've got places—houses— one in Miami, one in California, Hawaii. One over in Scotland. But you can never have too many of those."

She smiled. "Most people would be lucky to have just one."

"Unless you're in trouble and need it, then one is never enough," Levi said.

Bullard glanced at him. "Have you picked up any extras yet?"

"We're starting with safe houses first. The market in Texas has been up and down. But we found a couple good spots with cheap housing."

Bullard looked interested. "That's an idea. Safe houses. Such a government-espionage turn of phrase."

Several of the men grinned.

Brandon was interested. And these men had enough money to buy into the housing market. Their businesses must pay them well. Brandon was paid well, but it had never occurred to him that there was enough profit off the top to invest in things like this. At least in Levi's case, he funneled the money back into the company, one way or another. Putting in that pool, the size they were talking about, was no cheap project. Brandon looked at Bullard. "What's next for you?"

"Tidying up," he said. "There could be a shit ton of paperwork for the government with that gunrunning mess. I'm still fighting the drugs in my system. I'll need a couple days just to relax. I won't open my clinic for another few days. Then I'll see how I feel. But the more I was away, the more I realized how much I wanted to be home."

"Life is like that," Ice said. "It's not just about having somewhere to get away to. It's about making sure you have the right place to come home to."

Ice and Bullard shared a special smile, and Brandon could see how they were the best of good friends. She was completely comfortable beside Levi who didn't appear to be bothered in any way. That was the level of trust Brandon hoped to have with his partner one day. Speaking of that, he glanced at Kasha to see her laying her fork down gently and pushing away her plate. She sat back with the happy sigh. "Dave, that was absolutely lovely as usual."

Dave smiled. "You're always a pleasure to feed, my dear. You never complain, and you eat everything on your plate."

"It would be better if I didn't," she said. "But your cooking is so damn good." She stood and helped clear off the table.

Brandon contemplated the rest of the food and wondered if he should have seconds. Then he remembered Stone's comment about dessert. He glanced at Dave. "Is there dessert or should I have a second plate?"

Dave looked at him in surprise. "You should have a second plate *and* dessert." He picked up his load of dishes, turned and walked into the kitchen. Brandon looked at the food and nodded. "He's right. Why should I not avail myself of this bounty?" He dug in for a second round.

Chapter 13

KASHA HELPED DAVE in the kitchen. He kept shooing her away, but she refused. He motioned to the men outside. "It could be your last evening to spend with Brandon."

She shot him a sideways look. "And?"

He didn't say a word, but his quiet little knowing smile and eyes said enough.

She sighed. "Does everybody think I'm sweet on him?"

"Well, everybody knows he's sweet on *you*. The question is, is it mutual?"

She gave an irritated shrug. "He's leaving."

"And you're trying to leave," Dave said. "Does it really matter? You were looking for a place in the US. You have family in New Mexico. Levi's compound is only about forty-five minutes away from Houston."

"I don't know what I want to do," she said. "It's not like I can go without a job."

"You know there is one if you want it."

She put the last of the dishes into the dishwasher and turned, leaning against the counter. Dave was like a younger version of Alfred, she imagined. He was tall and lean and worked like a crazy man around this place. But he loved it. He also had a missing leg like Stone. The two men had adapted so well that she wondered if she would have even half the grace they did in the same circumstances. "In what capacity though?"

"What capacity do you want?" Levi asked, leaning against a doorway.

Kasha turned, feeling the heat roll up her cheeks. "I'm not even sure," she admitted. "I couldn't do a desk job."

"Maybe you should tell me what you prefer to do, and then we'll see how you would fit into the company."

She wrapped her fingers against the cupboard door. "I hate killing."

"That's a plus. Because nobody *should* like it," he said quietly.

She flung out her arm. "You know what I mean."

He nodded. "I do. And there's been a lot of it these last few days. But, speaking for myself, I haven't had to kill anyone in a long time before that," he admitted.

She studied him carefully. "Really?"

He nodded. "Really. We have a lot of women working for the company, and most don't go out on jobs. Except for Ice, who goes on missions with me."

"I'm not of Ice's caliber," she said.

He gave a warm chuckle. "Not many women are, but you're very close. So, if you want a job, I'd be happy to take you on. Give it three months, if you want, just for a trial. Maybe you'll get homesick and come back here to this ugly mug." He tilted his head toward Bullard, who was now leaning on the opposite side of the doorway.

She looked over at him and sighed. "Yes, that's part of the reason why I don't want to leave."

Bullard blustered, "Enough of that. We talked about it and decided it was time for you to go back to the US. For all you know, I'll open up another holding there."

She brightened. "Why would you do that?"

He chuckled and pointed toward Levi. "Because I'd be giving him a run for his money."

"But you could also share a company together. Levi could manage it with his men because he has more than you do apparently."

Bullard winced. "Okay, now that was a low blow."

"You're the one looking for mercenaries to help you out."

He raised both hands in mock surrender. "Okay, so staffing issues are a slight problem if you want to open up a second holding in Africa. But there are a lot of good men over here. They're landless, familyless, countryless. They need jobs and some focus."

"A lot of them are ex-military," Levi said.

"Which is most of what your crew is," she said.

Ice joined them at the doorway. "Maybe what you should ask is, what do you really want? We're happy to put you to work. Lord knows we're always looking for good men and women. With the bloody holidays right now, we've got people coming and going all the time. The staffing is a nightmare. We never know from one day to the next whether we'll have two or fourteen jobs and what kind of manpower we can count on."

"Now that would be a headache," Kasha said. "You know what I really like …" She stopped, self-conscious. "It's kind of stupid, considering I hate killing …"

"What?" Levi asked.

She glanced at Levi and Ice, who both remained unreadable, then at Bullard, but he had a smile playing around the corner of his lips as he leaned against the wall. The three of them together were such a power trio that she just couldn't imagine not working for at least one of them. There was just something special about being in their company. "I really like weapons," she admitted. "But it's stupid because I can't stand what they do."

"But you also recognize that, when they are needed, *not* having them is a death sentence."

"I hate the necessity of them, but it's the world we live in," she said. "I'm not a fool, and I'm not naive. But it would be my choice to never have to kill a human being again."

"So how do you feel about maiming?" Levi asked. There was no humor in his voice.

"I can maim just fine," she said drily. "Especially if they open their mouth and show what kind of an asshole they are."

Ice laughed out loud. "We have a lot of men working in active positions. But we don't have any field operatives who are women. Although Kai might be hired on, if we persuade her. She has her own business, so she'd only go out on the odd mission here and there. That goes for a couple other women at the compound too. But they're mostly specialists in forensic accounting, military self-defense, whatever. There are secondary roles we can put you into if you want. If no fieldwork is on your list, that's fine. We have lots of other work too."

"An office job would kill me," she said honestly. "I'm not sure what other secondary role you'd be talking about, unless it's helping Alfred. As much as I can handle a kitchen, I can't handle a kitchen full-time. Guys like Alfred and Dave are unbelievably talented at producing all the beautiful food they do."

Bullard said, "You're not taking Dave with you. Absolutely no way in hell am I suffering without him."

She shot him an innocent look and said, "I'm just going to steal him for a little while. Alfred's lonely."

Dave looked over at her and asked, "Is he?" There was immediate concern in his voice. "How do you know?"

She crossed her arms over her chest. "Alfred and I email back and forth," she said. "I like him. He's a sweetie."

Dave crossed his arms over his chest, mimicking her actions, and said, "What the hell am I then, chopped liver?"

She stretched up as far as she could to give him a kiss on the cheek. "You're a sweetheart. You're another reason I don't want to leave." Instantly his arms opened and came around her.

"We're setting up communications so, any time you want to talk to me, we'll have a television screen on both sides. I'll open up the monitors, and we can see into each other's lives on a regular basis."

She grinned. "Alfred would love that."

"And you?" Bullard asked. "How does that appeal to you, Kasha?"

"Maybe we should be asking Levi and Ice and the rest of the crew?"

"We are the ones who asked for it," Ice said. "The better the communication, the better we can collaborate, and the more cases we can work, so together we all are better off. Our companies aren't just about money. They're about doing the work we love to do, and, at the same time, helping countries badly ravaged by wars."

Kasha settled back, but Dave kept his arm around her shoulders. She really would miss him. Then she laughed out loud. "How can I possibly come if you don't have a swimming pool?"

Bullard nodded. "This girl is a swimming nut. She's in

two to three times a day, doing her laps."

"Good," Levi said. "As most of us are ex-SEALs, you can bet that, as soon as our pool is done, there'll be an awful lot of water play going on."

"How close are you to breaking ground?"

Ice broke into a big grin. "The pool is my pet project. We're breaking ground the minute I get my ass back to Texas."

After that, their conversation shifted to the type of filtration system she was putting in, the length of the pool and the extras to be added, how many stages the production and actual installation would take. Kasha felt a nudge from Dave. She glanced over to see him nodding toward the door, out to the pool area. She caught sight of Brandon leaning against the outside doorway—close enough to hear the conversation but far enough away that he wasn't part of it.

Dave leaned forward and said, "He doesn't want to affect your decision. But he sure is damn interested to see what you do." He squeezed her shoulder gently and said, "Go on. Put the guy out of his misery."

She snorted. "You're making this all up."

But it was a poor attempt to make light of something that obviously wasn't. She walked toward Brandon, stepping out into the last hour or so of the sunshine to see him leaning, his arms crossed over his chest and his eyes closed as if either slumbering or deep in thought. She stood beside him for a long moment, wondering if she should say anything.

"Well?" he asked softly.

"Maybe a three-month trial," she said hesitantly. "I'd really like to be able to come back and forth," she admitted. "I'm going to miss Bullard and Dave."

"I think that's a great idea. When you said you loved weapons, what do you mean by that?"

"I love maintaining them. I love taking them apart or cleaning them up. Keeping them stocked. Staying up on current prototypes. Ordering parts, ammo." She gave him a lopsided glance. "I look after all of Bullard's. To me they're just beautiful toys."

He studied her intently for a long moment. "Normally we all look after our own weapons. But we are building the armory. That could easily be an area for you to specialize in."

"An armory?"

He nodded. "It's a slow process. But it's going pretty well. When you add in specialized drones and some of the new training equipment we've got, they've done a hell of a job over there." He motioned around this old stone building with the big slow plantation fans and the almost dreamland-fantasy backyard. "It's not fancy like this. It's not as comfortable in the sense of, you know, the plantation-owner style of living. But what we've got is very special."

"You haven't been there all that long," she teased.

"Nope, I haven't. But I sure hope I get a chance to be there for a long time."

She stretched up the wall beside him, nudging him to move over a little bit to make room. "I'd been wondering about doing something completely different," she said. "But I'd miss parts of this."

"So maybe it's time to no longer do fieldwork. Or maybe do different kinds. We have work in many areas. Keep talking to Levi and Ice. What they really want is to see what you prefer to do because a happy person will do a much better job. If they put you into something that doesn't fit, then it's like sticking a round peg in a square hole, and that doesn't work so well."

"Does anybody ever feel like they're out of sorts? Like they don't quite fit? Like they're standing at a crossroads in their life, but they don't know which way to turn?"

"Well, that was me a few months ago. That was Rory who's not here right now. It was Michael too." Brandon reached out a hand and picked up hers so he could slide his fingers between hers. "I think it's everybody at some point in their lives. We get to a stage where we've done what we can do, and then we want something more. The trouble is, we don't know what the options are, so we take a step in one direction and hope it leads to better options."

"So you think I should take a step?" she asked with a chuckle.

"No, you should take several steps." He moved a little farther over and said, "Especially closer to me."

She turned to look at him. He grabbed her by the waist and tugged her gently so she leaned against him. They were hidden from the others in the kitchen, just tucked around the corner enough that they had some privacy.

"The thing is," she said, "I'd really like to get to know you better. But that's not reason enough to move to the US."

"No, it isn't," he said. "I'm sure I could come here and work for Bullard. But I just started with Levi," he added. "So that's not the best idea either."

She reared back slightly and looked at him. "Would you do that?"

He shrugged. "Well, it's kind of the same thing as what you are doing, isn't it? We don't want to let go of this. But, at the same time, there has to be a reason to change jobs. That's not a lightweight decision. I finally found something that makes me happy."

She nodded. "I've been planning on moving for a while. I told Bullard originally," she admitted, "that I would give him five years. It's been five years. But I'm not exactly sure what I want to do now."

"Then why not try Ice and Levi for three months? Take them up on their offer. Come to the US, and see how you feel about being back home again. If it doesn't work out, you know you've got a job with Bullard if you want it."

She chuckled. "I know he'd take me back."

"So then why not give it a try? Maybe work for them both? Just consider giving us a chance."

She stroked his cheek. "I never expected to meet somebody over here."

"But it's not really meeting somebody over *here*. It's about meeting," he corrected.

She thought about that for a long moment and then nodded. "That's very true. Still, it would be nice to know where this is going."

He slid his hand up the outside of her arm and slowly grasped her face. He said, "How about here." He tugged her forward and kissed her.

HE HADN'T INTENDED to take the kiss that far that fast. But there was something about having her in his arms. He'd worked beside her, watched her, worried about her and looked after her as well for such a short time, but it had been so intense, so real, like they had lived weeks in just a few days.

He didn't believe in instant attraction, but they'd already experienced so much. He knew he didn't want to let her go. No, he wasn't in love with her. At least he didn't think so.

But, if she didn't come back to the US with him, he wouldn't get a chance to find out what he really felt. Sure, he could ask Levi to let him go, so he could come here and work for Bullard. Brandon was pretty sure Bullard would take him on. Especially with the new holding. Back to full health with no side effects from the drugs, Bullard was making big plans. If he wanted in, he knew Bullard would be happy to let him in.

But Kasha wanted to come home again, so the most sensible thing would be for her to come to Levi and Ice's place. Only Brandon didn't want to influence her decision. Slowly he pulled back, knowing anybody could come around the corner. With one thumb, he gently stroked her cheekbone. Then he threw aside his good intentions and let his heart speak. "Come," he urged. "Let's give this a chance. Let's see what we have."

She chuckled gently. "I bet you say that to all the girls."

He gave her a slow dawning smile. "I haven't said that to anybody."

"Have you ever been in love?" she asked, her gaze searching.

He nodded. "Once or twice—at least I thought I was. Was it real? I don't know. None of my relationships lasted more than a year, so obviously they weren't meant to be."

"I haven't had any that lasted that long," she admitted.

"My ex-girlfriends didn't like me being away as much as I was. They hated not knowing if I was coming home from one day to the next."

"Aah, I can see that," she admitted. "That's not an issue for me."

"How would you feel if I was gone on missions?" he asked.

"How would you feel if *I* was gone on missions?" she asked him.

He gave a bark of laughter. "I don't know," he admitted. "It could be very hard."

She nodded. "It's a case of accepting who each other is and going on regardless."

Just then Levi stepped around the corner and, with a knowing look, said, "I know it's barely 8:00 p.m., but we're all crashing for the evening. We'll meet up again first thing in the morning at 6:00 a.m. to go over anything else that's needed before we fly home tomorrow." He looked at the two of them and said, "You guys might want to head to bed yourselves."

With a wink, he turned and walked away. Brandon could feel the laughter rolling up through his chest. It probably wasn't a good idea to let it out, but, when she chuckled, he grinned and couldn't stop.

She turned to look at him. "So, is that a hint of approval?"

"I don't know, but it was a suggestion. I don't know about you, but I'm all for it." He wrapped an arm around her shoulders and said, "Come on. If nothing else, we need sleep."

"If nothing else?" she asked in a dry tone.

He kissed her on the temple. "Sleep is a really good idea."

She nodded. "And do you mean that literally, or are you suggesting something else?"

He tugged her close and said, "I'm all for that."

She led him up the back stairs to a room he assumed was hers.

He stepped inside and looked around. Light wood, black

trim, lots of light with big windows. "I like this," he said appreciatively.

"I do too. It's been my room for five years."

She walked into the bathroom and closed the door gently in his face. He heard the toilet flush and then water run as she washed up. He wandered around her room, seeing so much of the other side of her. He had seen the tight black jeans, the tight T-shirts and the matching gun belts as well as the very capable hands handling semiautomatic machine guns. But he had yet to see her in the dresses hanging in the closet and wearing the high heels on the floor. Suddenly he couldn't wait to see that side of her. To see her out dancing in the moonlight—walking along a beach, holding hands, in nothing but a bikini. There was such a big world out there. He wanted to see it with her. They hadn't had any time to really get to know each other. But they'd known each other in so many ways that counted. When she didn't come right back out, he got worried. He knocked on the door and said, "Are you okay?"

She chuckled and said, "The question is, are you?"

She opened the door, and his heart almost fell to his toes. Tall, lean, high firm breasts, narrow waist, beautiful hips and long legs.

All of it nude in front of him.

His breath caught in the back of his throat, and he tried to say something, but it came out as a croak.

She took a step forward and said, "I always sleep in the nude." She walked over to the bed, pulled back the bedding and got in. "Are you coming to sleep or not?"

He shook his head. But his hands were moving as fast as they could as they unbuttoned and unzipped until he was stripped down the same as she was. "I was kind of thinking of a shower."

"I was too. But I'm tired. I figured afterward."

There was such a suggestive tone to her voice, but still, he wasn't exactly sure. "Afterward? You mean, when we wake up?"

She opened her eyes and gave him a sloe-eyed look that had his body coming awake and fast. He walked around to his side of the bed and crawled in under the covers. He almost groaned at the cool sheets sliding over his skin. He was exhausted and sore.

She rolled over and said, "Sleep first. We will enjoy it so much more when we wake up."

She shifted backward until they were spooning, and, within seconds, he could hear her long slow breaths as she fell asleep in his arms. He wondered at a woman with the self-confidence to do what she had just done, and the security to just fall asleep in his arms. He tucked her up closer and closed his eyes and fell asleep too.

He woke several hours later to moonlight streaming into the room and an empty bed. He stared at the indent in the pillow beside him and swore softly. He sat up and realized water was running. She'd gotten up and gone into the shower. He checked the clock on her night table. He'd slept for almost five full hours. Not enough to replenish his lack of sleep over the last couple days or to go out on a twelve-mile run but enough that he could make it through the rest of the day if need be. It also meant he had a full five hours before they were supposed to meet up with everybody. He slid out of bed and walked into the bathroom.

Through the glass walls, he could see her standing under the showerhead. Just standing there, her face lifted to the full force of the water, letting the shower sluice down her hair and back. It was a stunningly beautiful picture of complete natural beauty. Completely unselfconscious. She just enjoyed the moment. It took him a longer moment to realize she had her hand out, reaching for him. He stepped forward. The glass door slid open, letting him step inside.

She turned and smiled. "Shower time."

She made room so he could step in under the huge rain head. He turned his face up against the water, relishing the warmth and the soothing heat as it stroked his head and ran down his back. While he stood there, enjoying the moment, he felt a bar of soap slide over his skin. He opened his eyes and stared at her in surprise.

"Never been washed before?" she asked in a teasing voice.

He shook his head. "No, I don't think I have been. I would have remembered that."

Not only did she wash him but she scrubbed him with a natural bristle brush. It felt so damn good as she worked over his back and his shoulders and his chest. By the time she was done, his skin felt invigorated and alive.

"That's almost as good as a couple hours' sleep," he murmured.

She handed him the shampoo bottle.

He washed his hair and then turned to help her with her long hair. She kept it in a braid most of the day. But now that it was undone, it was partially tangled. After shampooing it, he worked in conditioner, and then, with a large-toothed comb, he gently untangled it. By the time they were done, he was amazed at the naturalness of being with her. He wasn't used to that. He would have made love the first time he hit the bed with anyone else. He would have made love in the shower with anyone else.

But she was still treating him as a friend. Obviously a close friend and, so far, ignoring his obvious physical reaction to her. But they hadn't crossed that line. He wasn't sure if she was holding back or if she was raising his anticipation levels on purpose. When she turned to rinse the last of the conditioner out of her hair, she slid her arms up around his neck and kissed him. He pulled her tight, skin to skin, their hot wet slick bodies still soapy, and held her close. She was a perfect fit. He was tall but not supertall like some of the men. He was big, but he wasn't a monster like Stone. And she just seemed to fit … everywhere.

He groaned, feeling his body temperature rising. It felt too incredible to move. He wanted to take her to bed, but, at the same time, he didn't want to leave the warm water. Thoughts of the hot tub came to mind. But obviously not in somebody else's house and certainly not when full of other people. She pulled back slightly and murmured, "I have been wanting to do that since forever."

He glanced down at her in surprise. "What? Kiss me?"

"Kiss you in the shower," she corrected. "I'm a water baby." This time she pulled him down so she could nibble on his lips, his chin, kiss his cheeks and run white silky fingers over his closed eyes, forehead, and then through his scalp.

"There's just nothing like water," she added gently. Her hand stroked down his arms, his chest, his hips. When she enclosed his erection, he moaned softly, a shudder working from deep inside up and out through his body.

She chuckled and said, "I've been wanting to meet this guy for a long time."

Her humor lightened the atmosphere and at the same time raised the temperature that much more. Something else he wasn't used to. But it felt right. It felt natural. Matter of fact, it felt damn good.

He grabbed the bar of soap. "My turn," he whispered as he dragged the soap across her breasts, cupping first one firmly with his hand and then the other, the bar gently teasing as he soaped her from head to toe. Unable to help himself, he pulled her back against him, his hands reaching around to cup her breasts, then to slide down to tangle at the juncture of her thighs. She moaned, arching into his fingers. Gently he slid one finger deeper into the soft skin folds to the button hidden within. She cried out, the soap making her even more slippery against him. She turned him and pivoted so she was up against the back wall, and the water now pounded on his back. She slipped her arms around him and said, "I really don't want to wait."

Again it amazed him. She was just so damn natural about all this. A nymph in the water and everything seemed normal. More than normal, it seemed right. She lifted one leg high up over his hip and gently rubbed against him. He reached down and caught both of her back cheeks and pressed her against the wall. But he wasn't ready to take this to the limit already. He wanted to enjoy the moment. Enjoy having her in his arms.

He kissed her again—slow, drugging, tongue-stroking, passion-fueling kisses—even as his fingers continued to tease her. He squeezed her buttocks tight, holding her firmly—yet holding off. With both her legs wrapped around his hips, she rocked back and forth as she clutched at his head and held him firm for her kiss. Tongues danced, fingers stroked, and all the while the temperature of the water added to the steaminess. Finally he couldn't stand it. He pulled back, arched and filled her completely.

She cried out and lay pinned against the wall, shuddering.

He waited a long moment and murmured against her ear, "Are you okay?"

She shook her head. "No, I'm not."

He pulled back ever-so-slightly, looked at her in surprise.

She said, "But I will be if you start to move." She pinched his buttocks.

He gave a shout of laughter and plunged deep. Once would never be enough. He held her tight, kept her pressed against the wall so she wouldn't fall and pounded, driving them both to the cliff's edge they so desperately wanted. When she came apart in his arms, he rode her through it. Then, with a long, low groan, he felt his whole body clench as his climax ripped through him.

He laid his head against the wall for a long moment. Her hands gently stroked his back. He reached down and kissed her neck. But that was about as much effort as he could expend. Slowly she disengaged herself and shifted so they were both in the full spray of the water, and then finally she shut it off. She grabbed two towels and said, "We have plenty of time yet. Let's go back to bed."

Again following, he stepped out, wrapped one towel around his hips and used the other to dry off. As they walked into the bedroom, moonlight fell across the bed. She laughed and said, "I love that about it here. The sunshine is nice too in this room, especially in the afternoon, if I could just lie in bed during that time, not that I ever got much chance to do that," she admitted. "But it's just such a special light that hits this bedroom."

The bed was still warm from when they had left it. She sat down and gently towel-dried her hair. He dried off and sat beside her and then took over the job of separating her long locks and squeezing out the excess moisture. When he was done, she shifted until she sat in his lap and looped her arms around his neck. "I wish we were already in the US."

He looked at her in surprise. "Are you sure you want to come?"

She nodded. "I'm sure. Like you, I want to see where this goes. I've never felt anything so special in my life."

He wrapped his arms around her and just held her close. "I don't know what to call this," he admitted. "I'm scared to jump to conclusions and make more of it than it is. But, at the same time, I'm petrified I'll lose you."

She tilted his chin up and dropped a light kiss on his lips. "I don't have any intention of losing you. So, whether we stay here or we go back to Levi's, it doesn't really matter. I always did intend to go back home again though. I have a lot of family in New Mexico. They are expecting me."

"Is New Mexico a place you want to visit, or are you planning on moving back there?"

"A place to visit. I think I'll give Levi and Ice's offer a chance. See where we are in three months. Maybe talk to Bullard too about coming back here if I want to later," she admitted. "Are you good with that?"

He smiled as her fingers stroked his cheek. He kissed each one. "I'm more than good with that. I'm really thrilled at that idea." He crushed her against him, his lips sealing the deal for now and hopefully forever. He knew the guys would tease him. They had yet to have a relationship break up at Legendary Security. That was part of what made the company and all its people so legendary. He wouldn't have believed it if he hadn't seen it for himself. He wanted that. Maybe, if he was lucky, he had found it.

"Let's make love again," she said, as she lay back on the bed with a lazy sigh.

"With pleasure," Brandon said, kissing her deeply.

AFTER THEIR LOVEMAKING, they both dozed for another couple hours. When she woke up, she checked the time.

He chuckled. "It's only 5:00 a.m. We're not late for the meeting. But we do have more time just for us."

She leaned over and looked at him with a smile and said, "You know we can make it if we want to."

"I want to," he whispered. "I want it all."

Her eyes darkened, and her lips pouted. She gently bit him on the bottom lip and whispered, "So do I. How about we take one step at a time and see where we end up?" She nipped him again gently and asked, "Is that a deal?"

He lifted her chin and whispered, "It's a deal."

He kissed her. Not just for the moment, not just for the hour, not just for the day. But, if he was a lucky man, it would be forever.

Epilogue

LIAM O'BRIEN STEPPED to the side, peering out the garage window, watching as Brandon parked nearby. Rory and Michael stood at Liam's side as they watched their friend arrive with Kasha. They'd heard from Ice how crazy saving Bullard had been and how it had ended up with another of their own finding a partner.

"Told you, Liam. Our unit is all here," Michael said quietly at his side.

"And, except for you, we're all taken," Rory added to Michael's comment.

"And it's a good thing too," Michael said. "We were all lost for long enough. I never thought to find anyone who'd accept me or put up with me. But it's all good." He slapped Liam on the shoulder.

"I'm not sure I'm ready for this," Liam admitted. "It's one thing to be a part of this family thing you guys have going on, but it's a completely different issue to be standing on the outside and looking in. I'm not sure there's a place for me here. And, even if there is, I'd have no idea how to fit in."

"That's the thing. None of us did before we arrived. You have to trust you'll find your way."

Just then Brandon got out of the truck and stretched.

Damn, he looked good. Liam had been close to him—

Rory and Michael too—but there'd always been a connection between Liam and Brandon. And to see his buddy looking so happy, ... so fit—both emotionally and physically—well, it was a joy.

Liam would love and accept Kasha for that alone. They'd all had a hell of a last year. Each one in their unit had moved past it in their own way. Except for Liam.

The happy couple was laughing and talking as they moved toward the kitchen door. Liam could hear their conversation.

"It's a good thing we took a week off before coming here." Kasha beamed at Brandon.

He chuckled. "In truth that week was like a minihoneymoon."

Liam grinned at the flags of color blooming on Kasha's cheeks, but she didn't hide them. Instead she nodded. "It was indeed. It was also nice to see my family."

The huge double doors opened then. Liam glanced at Levi who was manning the controls on the garage. Levi waited for the door to lift fully, then stepped out.

"So much for being here when I arrived." Liam grinned at the blank look on Brandon's face before it lit up in joy.

The two men hugged each other.

Brandon stepped back to study Liam's face. "When the hell did you get here? You said you were considering it, not that you'd made up your mind." He slugged Liam on his shoulder. "Damn, it's good to see you."

"You haven't missed me at all," Liam scoffed, nodding to the stunning woman at Brandon's side.

"This is Kasha." Brandon held out his arm for her. She stepped close enough that his arm slid around her shoulder. "Kasha, this is my good friend, Liam. He and I were in the same unit in the navy."

The smile Kasha flashed his way was both delightful and compassionate. Enough for him to know Brandon obviously cared a lot about this woman if he'd shared some of these last few years' events.

He shook her hand. "Nice to meet you." He'd heard plenty about Kasha and Bullard and the nightmare Levi's team had gone through as they'd flown over to help out in Africa. "Too bad I didn't meet you first," he said in a teasing tone.

"There's a reason I overwhelmed her with my charms so fast." Brandon laughed. "You have a reputation with women …"

Kasha laughed. Liam gave her a lopsided grin, and her eyes widened. "Wow, that's a lethal smile."

Brandon tugged her close. "See?" he complained. "Women drop at his feet."

She sent Brandon a sideways glance. "I'm still standing."

He leaned over and kissed her. Then they both broke out laughing.

Just then Levi and Ice walked over. Ice smiled and said, "About time you two got here. We've got a crapload of work to do."

More of the clan arrived to greet the newcomers. Liam still struggled to remember everyone's name, and he'd been here a week already.

But Kasha walked in confidently, shaking hands with those she didn't know as she introduced herself.

"A lot of new faces are around here," Levi said to Liam.

"It'll take me time to learn everybody's name," Liam replied.

Levi finished the introductions. He turned to both

Brandon and Rory and said, "You guys up for work? We weren't kidding about the jobs. We've caught several hot ones this morning alone."

Both men nodded, their faces brightening with interest. "We are so ready."

Levi turned to Kasha and said, "Are you on field duty or office work?"

She snorted. "Am I dead yet?"

Ice laughed. "That's my girl."

Levi gave her a wide smile and said, "Welcome. And goodbye. All three of you are leaving in the morning."

Liam looked from one to the other with a big smile and said, "What about me? Do you have something for me?" He'd done one short security job for Levi since he'd arrived, but, other than that, Liam had been helping set up the new security-alarm-system side of the business. That had been fun as he'd gotten to know several of the locals and had enjoyed being around the animals at Anna and Flynn's place. Then the puppies at the compound were adorable too. He was afraid to care and get his heart broken when they were adopted out—if they were adopted out. Something he knew Alfred and Bailey were fighting pretty hard against.

Levi chuckled. "If you want to go out on this one, you've got it."

Liam nodded. "I'm in."

"Be ready to leave by 6:00 a.m."

There was a collective groan but not from Liam. He was energized. "That's awesome. Where are we going? Somewhere exotic, like Thailand? Maybe a sandy paradise, like the Sahara? How about foggy Scotland?"

Ice, standing in the doorway, called out, "How about horses in Texas?"

He turned to her and said, "But we're in Texas now. There's nothing exotic about that."

She grinned. "Just you wait. There's something very exotic ahead for you."

On that cryptic note, she walked back inside, leaving Liam staring at her. He wasn't exactly sure what she meant by that.

Levi smacked him on the shoulder and said, "Don't worry about it. Ice is good at this sort of stuff."

Liam looked at him suspiciously. "What sort of stuff?"

But Levi was already stepping inside the house. He tossed back, "You'll find out soon enough. Just keep an open mind—and heart—and you'll be good."

At the open-heart comment, the others grinned, then laughed. Liam stared at them. "What the hell did he mean by that?"

Everyone just walked away, some laughing, others whistling.

Liam glared at Brandon, waiting for clarification.

Brandon shrugged and said, "Trust me. Like Levi said, you'll find out soon enough."

Then Brandon walked inside with Kasha, leaving Liam alone to contemplate what everyone else already knew, and he had yet to find out.

This concludes Book 13 of Heroes for Hire: Brandon's Bliss.

Read about Liam's Lily: Heroes for Hire, Book 14

Heroes for Hire: Liam's Lily
(Book #14)

Welcome to Liam's Lily, book 14 in Heroes for Hire, reconnecting readers with the unforgettable men from SEALs of Honor in a new series of action-packed, page turning romantic suspense that fans have come to expect from USA TODAY Bestselling author Dale Mayer.

Book 14 is available now!
To find out more visit Dale Mayer's website.
https://geni.us/DMliamUniversal

Other Military Series by Dale Mayer

SEALs of Honor

Heroes for Hire

SEALs of Steel

The K9 Files

The Mavericks

Bullards Battle

Hathaway House

Terkel's Team

Ryland's Reach: Bullard's Battle (Book #1)

Welcome to a new stand-alone but interconnected series from Dale Mayer. This is Bullard's story—and that of his team's. All raw, rough, incredibly capable men who have one goal: to find out who was behind the attack on their leader, before the attacker, or attackers, return to finish the job.

Stay tuned for more nonstop action as the men narrow down their suspects … and find a way to let love back into their own empty lives.

His rescue from the ocean after a horrible plane explosion was his top priority, in any way, shape, or form. A small sailboat and a nurse to do the job was more than Ryland hoped for.

When Tabi somehow drags him and his buddy Garret onboard and surprisingly gets them to a naval ship close by, Ryland figures he'd used up all his luck and his friend's too. Sure enough, those who attacked the plane they were in weren't content to let him slowly die in the ocean. No. Surviving had made him a target all over again.

Tabi isn't expecting her sailing holiday to include the rescue of two badly injured men and then to end with the loss of her beloved sailboat. Her instincts save them, but now she finds it tough to let them go—even as more of Bullard's team members come to them—until it becomes apparent that not only are Bullard and his men still targets ... but she is too.

B ULLARD CHECKED THAT the helicopter was loaded with their bags and that his men were ready to leave.

He walked back one more time, his gaze on Ice. She'd never looked happier, never looked more perfect. His heart ached, but he knew she remained a caring friend and always would be. He opened his arms; she ran into them, and he held her close, whispering, "The offer still stands."

She leaned back and smiled up at him. "Maybe if and when Levi's been gone for a long enough time for me to forget," she said in all seriousness.

"That's not happening. You two, now three, will live long and happy lives together," he said, smiling down at the woman knew to be the most beautiful, inside and out. She would never be his, but he always kept a little corner of his heart open and available, in case she wanted to surprise him and to slide inside.

And then he realized she'd already been a part of his heart all this time. That was a good ten to fifteen years by now. But she kept herself in the friend category, and he understood because she and Levi, partners and now parents, were perfect together.

Bullard reached out and shook Levi's hand. "It was a hell of a blast," he said. "When you guys do a big splash, you really do a *big* splash."

Ice laughed. "A few days at home sounds perfect for me now."

"It looks great," he said, his hands on his hips as he surveyed the people in the massive pool surrounded by the palm trees, all designed and decked out by Ice. Right beside all the war machines that he heartily approved of. He grinned at her. "When are you coming over to visit?" His gaze went to Levi, raising his eyebrows back at her. "You guys should come over for a week or two or three."

"It's not a bad idea," Levi said. "We could use a long holiday, just not yet."

"That sounds familiar." Bullard grinned. "Anyway, I'm off. We'll hit the airport and then pick up the plane and head home." He added, "As always, call if you need me."

Everybody raised a hand as he returned to the helicopter and his buddy who was flying him to the airport. Ice had volunteered to shuttle him there, but he hadn't wanted to take her away from her family or to prolong the goodbye. He hopped inside, waving at everybody as the helicopter lifted. Two of his men, Ryland and Garret, were in the back seats. They always traveled with him.

Bullard would pick up the rest of his men in Australia. He stared down at the compound as he flew overhead. He preferred his compound at home, but damn they'd done a nice job here.

With everybody on the ground screaming goodbye, Bullard sailed over Houston, heading toward the airport. His two men never said a word. They all knew how he felt about Ice. But not one of them would cross that line and say anything. At least not if they expected to still have jobs.

It was one thing to fall in love with another man's woman, but another thing to fall in love with a woman who was so unique, so different, and so absolutely perfect that you knew, just knew, there was no hope of finding anybody else like her. But she and Levi had been together way before Bullard had ever met her, which made it that much more heartbreaking.

Still, he'd turned and looked forward. He had a full roster of jobs himself to focus on when he got home. Part of him was tired of the life; another part of him couldn't wait to head out on the next adventure. He managed to run everything from his command centers in one or two of his locations. He'd spent a lot of time and effort at the second one and kept a full team at both locations, yet preferred to spend most of his time at the old one. It felt more like home to him, and he'd like to be there now, but still had many more days before that could happen.

The helicopter lowered to the tarmac, he stepped out, said his goodbyes and walked across to where his private plane waited. It was one of the things that he loved, being a pilot of both helicopters and airplanes, and owning both birds himself.

That again was another way he and Ice were part of the same team, of the same mind-set. He'd been looking for another woman like Ice for himself, but no such luck. Sure, lots were around for short-term relationships, but most of them couldn't handle his lifestyle or the violence of the world that he lived in. He understood that.

The ones who did had a hard edge to them that he found difficult to live with. Bullard appreciated everybody's being alert and aware, but if there wasn't some softness in the women, they seemed to turn cold all the way through.

As he boarded his small plane, Ryland and Garret following behind, Bullard called out in his loud voice, "Let's go, slow pokes. We've got a long flight ahead of us."

The men grinned, confident Bullard was teasing, as was his usual routine during their off-hours.

"Well, we're ready, not sure about you though …" Ryland said, smirking.

"We're waiting on you this time," Garret added with a chuckle. "Good thing you're the boss."

Bullard grinned at his two right-hand men. "Isn't that the truth?" He dropped his bags at one of the guys' feet and said, "Stow all this stuff, will you? I want to get our flight path cleared and get the hell out of here."

They'd all enjoyed the break. He tried to get over once a year to visit Ice and Levi and same in reverse. But it was time to get back to business. He started up the engines, got confirmation from the tower. They were heading to Australia for this next job. He really wanted to go straight back to Africa, but it would be a while yet. They'd refuel in Honolulu.

Ryland came in and sat down in the copilot's spot, buckled in, then asked, "You ready?"

Bullard laughed. "When have you ever known me *not* to be ready?" At that, he taxied down the runway. Before long he was up in the air, at cruising level, and heading to Hawaii. "Gotta love these views from up here," Bullard said. "This place is magical."

"It is once you get up above all the smog," he said. "Why Australia again?"

"Remember how we were supposed to check out that newest compound in Australia that I've had my eye on? Besides the alpha team is coming off that ugly job in Sydney. We'll give them a day or two of R&R then head home."

"Right. We could have some equally ugly payback on that job."

Bullard shrugged. "That goes for most of our jobs. It's the life."

"And don't you have enough compounds to look after?"

"Yes I do, but that kid in me still looks to take over the world. Just remember that."

"Better you go home to Africa and look after your first two compounds," Ryland said.

"Maybe," Bullard admitted. "But it seems hard to not continue expanding."

"You need a partner," Ryland said abruptly. "That might ease the savage beast inside. Keep you home more."

"Well, the only one I like," he said, "is married to my best friend."

"I'm sorry about that," Ryland said quietly. "What a shit deal."

"No," Bullard said. "I came on the scene last. They were always meant to be together. Especially now they are a family."

"If you say so," Ryland said.

Bullard nodded. "Damn right, I say so."

And that set the tone for the next many hours. They landed in Hawaii, and while they fueled up everybody got off to stretch their legs by walking around outside a bit as this was a small private airstrip, not exactly full of hangars and tourists. Then they hopped back on board again for takeoff.

"I can fly," Ryland offered as they took off.

"We'll switch in a bit," Bullard said. "Surprisingly, I'm doing okay yet, but I'll let you take her down."

"Yeah, it's still a long flight," Ryland said studying the islands below. It was a stunning view of the area.

"I love the islands here. Sometimes I just wonder about the benefit of, you know, crashing into the sea, coming up on a deserted island, and finding the simple life again," Bullard said with a laugh.

"I hear you," Ryland said. "Every once in a while, I wonder the same."

Several hours later Ryland looked up and said abruptly, "We've made good time considering we've already passed Fiji."

Bullard yawned.

"Let's switch."

Bullard smiled, nodded, and said, "Fine. I'll hand it over to you."

Just then a funny noise came from the engine on the right side.

They looked at each other, and Ryland said, "Uh-oh. That's not good news."

Boom!

And the plane exploded.

Find Bullard's Battle (Book #1) here!

To find out more visit Dale Mayer's website.

https://geni.us/DMRylandUniversal

Damon's Deal: Terkel's Team (Book #1)

Welcome to a brand-new connected series of intrigue, betrayal, and ... murder, from the *USA Today* best-selling author Dale Mayer. A series with all the elements you've come to love, plus so much more... including psychics!

A betrayal from within has Terkel frantic to protect those he can, as his team falls one by one, from a murderous killer he helped create.

ICE POURED HERSELF a coffee and sat down at the compound's massive dining room table with the others. When her phone rang, she smiled at the number displayed. "Hey, Terk. How're you doing?" She put the call on Speakerphone.

"I'm okay," Terkel said, his voice distracted and tight.

"Terk?" Merk called from across the table. He got up and walked closer and sat across from Levi. "You don't sound too good, brother. What's up?"

"I'm fine," Terk said. "Or I will be. Right now, things are blown to shit."

"As in literally?" Merk asked.

"The entire group," Terk said, "they're all gone. I had a solid team of eight, and they're all gone."

"Dead?"

Several others stood to join them, gathered around Ice's phone. Levi stepped forward, his hand on Ice's shoulder. "Terk? Are they all dead?"

"No." Terk took a deep breath. "I'm not making sense. I'm sorry."

"Take it easy," Ice said, her voice calm and reassuring. "What do you mean, *they're all gone?*"

"All their abilities are gone," he said. "Something's happened to them. Somebody has deliberately removed whatever super senses they could utilize—or what we have been utilizing for the last ten years for the government." His tone was bitter. "When the US gov recently closed us down, they promised that our black ops department would never rise again, but I didn't expect them to attack us personally."

"What are you talking about?" Merk said in alarm, standing up now to stare at Ice's phone. "Are you in danger?"

"Maybe? I don't know," Terk said. "I need to find out exactly what the hell's going on."

"What can we do to help?" Ice asked.

Terk gave a broken laugh. "That's not why I'm calling. Well, it is, but it isn't."

Ice looked at Merk, who frowned, as he shook his head. Ice knew he and the others had heard Terk's stressed out tone and the completely confusing bits and pieces coming from his mouth. Ice said, "Terk, you're not making sense again. Take a breath and explain. Please. You're scaring me."

Terk took a long slow deep breath. "Tell Stone to open the gate," he said. "She's out there."

"Who's out there?" Levi asked, hopped up, looked outside, and shrugged.

"She's coming up the road now. You have to let her in."

"Who? Why?"

"*Because*," he said, "she's also harnessed with C-4."

"Jesus," Levi said, bolting to display the camera feeds to the big screen in the room. "Is it live?"

"It is, and she's been sent to you."

"Well, that's an interesting move," Ice said, her voice sharp, activating her comm to connect to Stone in the control room. "Who's after us?"

"I think it's rebels within the Iranian government. But it could be our own government. I don't know anymore," Terk snapped. "I also don't know how they got her so close to you. Or how they pinned your connection to me," he said. "I've been very careful."

"We can look after ourselves," Ice said immediately. "But who is this woman to you?"

"She's pregnant," he said, "so that adds to the intensity here."

"Understood. So who is the father? Is he connected somehow?"

There was silence on the other end.

Merk said, "Terk, talk to us."

"She's carrying my baby," Terk replied, his voice heavy.

Merk, his expression grim, looked at Ice, her face mirroring his shock. He asked, "How do you know her, Terk?"

"Brother, you don't understand," Terk said. "I've never met this woman before in my life." And, with that, the phone went dead.

Find Terkel's Team (Book #1) here!

To find out more visit Dale Mayer's website.

https://geni.us/DMTTDamonUniversal

Author's Note

Thank you for reading Brandon's Bliss: Heroes for Hire, Book 13! If you enjoyed the book, please take a moment and leave a short review.

Dear reader,

I love to hear from readers, and you can contact me at my website: www.dalemayer.com or at my Facebook author page. To be informed of new releases and special offers, sign up for my newsletter or follow me on BookBub. And if you are interested in joining Dale Mayer's Reader Group, here is the Facebook sign up page.
http://geni.us/DaleMayerFBGroup

Cheers,
Dale Mayer

About the Author

Dale Mayer is a *USA Today* best-selling author, best known for her SEALs military romances, her Psychic Visions series, and her Lovely Lethal Garden cozy series. Her contemporary romances are raw and full of passion and emotion (Broken But ... Mending, Hathaway House series). Her thrillers will keep you guessing (Kate Morgan, By Death series), and her romantic comedies will keep you giggling (*It's a Dog's Life*, a stand-alone novella; and the Broken Protocols series, starring Charming Marvin, the cat).

Dale honors the stories that come to her—and some of them are crazy, break all the rules and cross multiple genres!

To go with her fiction, she also writes nonfiction in many different fields, with books available on résumé writing, companion gardening, and the US mortgage system. All her books are available in print and ebook format.

Connect with Dale Mayer Online

Dale's Website – www.dalemayer.com
Twitter – @DaleMayer
Facebook Page – geni.us/DaleMayerFBFanPage
Facebook Group – geni.us/DaleMayerFBGroup
BookBub – geni.us/DaleMayerBookbub
Instagram – geni.us/DaleMayerInstagram
Goodreads – geni.us/DaleMayerGoodreads
Newsletter – geni.us/DaleNews

Also by Dale Mayer

Published Adult Books:

Bullard's Battle
Ryland's Reach, Book 1
Cain's Cross, Book 2
Eton's Escape, Book 3
Garret's Gambit, Book 4
Kano's Keep, Book 5
Fallon's Flaw, Book 6
Quinn's Quest, Book 7
Bullard's Beauty, Book 8
Bullard's Best, Book 9

Terkel's Team
Damon's Deal, Book 1

Kate Morgan
Simon Says... Hide, Book 1

Hathaway House
Aaron, Book 1
Brock, Book 2
Cole, Book 3
Denton, Book 4
Elliot, Book 5
Finn, Book 6

Gregory, Book 7

Heath, Book 8

Iain, Book 9

Jaden, Book 10

Keith, Book 11

Lance, Book 12

Melissa, Book 13

Nash, Book 14

Owen, Book 15

Hathaway House, Books 1–3

Hathaway House, Books 4–6

Hathaway House, Books 7–9

The K9 Files

Ethan, Book 1

Pierce, Book 2

Zane, Book 3

Blaze, Book 4

Lucas, Book 5

Parker, Book 6

Carter, Book 7

Weston, Book 8

Greyson, Book 9

Rowan, Book 10

Caleb, Book 11

Kurt, Book 12

Tucker, Book 13

Harley, Book 14

The K9 Files, Books 1–2

The K9 Files, Books 3–4

The K9 Files, Books 5–6

The K9 Files, Books 7–8

The K9 Files, Books 9–10
The K9 Files, Books 11–12

Lovely Lethal Gardens
Arsenic in the Azaleas, Book 1
Bones in the Begonias, Book 2
Corpse in the Carnations, Book 3
Daggers in the Dahlias, Book 4
Evidence in the Echinacea, Book 5
Footprints in the Ferns, Book 6
Gun in the Gardenias, Book 7
Handcuffs in the Heather, Book 8
Ice Pick in the Ivy, Book 9
Jewels in the Juniper, Book 10
Killer in the Kiwis, Book 11
Lifeless in the Lilies, Book 12
Murder in the Marigolds, Book 13
Lovely Lethal Gardens, Books 1–2
Lovely Lethal Gardens, Books 3–4
Lovely Lethal Gardens, Books 5–6
Lovely Lethal Gardens, Books 7–8
Lovely Lethal Gardens, Books 9–10

Psychic Vision Series
Tuesday's Child
Hide 'n Go Seek
Maddy's Floor
Garden of Sorrow
Knock Knock…
Rare Find
Eyes to the Soul
Now You See Her

Shattered
Into the Abyss
Seeds of Malice
Eye of the Falcon
Itsy-Bitsy Spider
Unmasked
Deep Beneath
From the Ashes
Stroke of Death
Ice Maiden
Snap, Crackle…
Psychic Visions Books 1–3
Psychic Visions Books 4–6
Psychic Visions Books 7–9

By Death Series
Touched by Death
Haunted by Death
Chilled by Death
By Death Books 1–3

Broken Protocols – Romantic Comedy Series
Cat's Meow
Cat's Pajamas
Cat's Cradle
Cat's Claus
Broken Protocols 1-4

Broken and… Mending
Skin
Scars
Scales (of Justice)

Broken but... Mending 1-3

Glory
Genesis
Tori
Celeste
Glory Trilogy

Biker Blues
Morgan: Biker Blues, Volume 1
Cash: Biker Blues, Volume 2

SEALs of Honor
Mason: SEALs of Honor, Book 1
Hawk: SEALs of Honor, Book 2
Dane: SEALs of Honor, Book 3
Swede: SEALs of Honor, Book 4
Shadow: SEALs of Honor, Book 5
Cooper: SEALs of Honor, Book 6
Markus: SEALs of Honor, Book 7
Evan: SEALs of Honor, Book 8
Mason's Wish: SEALs of Honor, Book 9
Chase: SEALs of Honor, Book 10
Brett: SEALs of Honor, Book 11
Devlin: SEALs of Honor, Book 12
Easton: SEALs of Honor, Book 13
Ryder: SEALs of Honor, Book 14
Macklin: SEALs of Honor, Book 15
Corey: SEALs of Honor, Book 16
Warrick: SEALs of Honor, Book 17
Tanner: SEALs of Honor, Book 18
Jackson: SEALs of Honor, Book 19

Kanen: SEALs of Honor, Book 20
Nelson: SEALs of Honor, Book 21
Taylor: SEALs of Honor, Book 22
Colton: SEALs of Honor, Book 23
Troy: SEALs of Honor, Book 24
Axel: SEALs of Honor, Book 25
Baylor: SEALs of Honor, Book 26
Hudson: SEALs of Honor, Book 27
SEALs of Honor, Books 1–3
SEALs of Honor, Books 4–6
SEALs of Honor, Books 7–10
SEALs of Honor, Books 11–13
SEALs of Honor, Books 14–16
SEALs of Honor, Books 17–19
SEALs of Honor, Books 20–22
SEALs of Honor, Books 23–25

Heroes for Hire

Levi's Legend: Heroes for Hire, Book 1
Stone's Surrender: Heroes for Hire, Book 2
Merk's Mistake: Heroes for Hire, Book 3
Rhodes's Reward: Heroes for Hire, Book 4
Flynn's Firecracker: Heroes for Hire, Book 5
Logan's Light: Heroes for Hire, Book 6
Harrison's Heart: Heroes for Hire, Book 7
Saul's Sweetheart: Heroes for Hire, Book 8
Dakota's Delight: Heroes for Hire, Book 9
Tyson's Treasure: Heroes for Hire, Book 10
Jace's Jewel: Heroes for Hire, Book 11
Rory's Rose: Heroes for Hire, Book 12
Brandon's Bliss: Heroes for Hire, Book 13
Liam's Lily: Heroes for Hire, Book 14

SEALs of Steel

The Mavericks

Collections

Standalone Novellas

Published Young Adult Books:

Family Blood Ties Series
Vampire in Denial
Vampire in Distress
Vampire in Design
Vampire in Deceit
Vampire in Defiance
Vampire in Conflict
Vampire in Chaos
Vampire in Crisis
Vampire in Control
Vampire in Charge
Family Blood Ties Set 1–3
Family Blood Ties Set 1–5
Family Blood Ties Set 4–6
Family Blood Ties Set 7–9
Sian's Solution, A Family Blood Ties Series Prequel
    Novelette

Design series
Dangerous Designs
Deadly Designs
Darkest Designs
Design Series Trilogy

Standalone
In Cassie's Corner
Gem Stone (a Gemma Stone Mystery)
Time Thieves

Published Non-Fiction Books:

Career Essentials

Career Essentials: The Résumé
Career Essentials: The Cover Letter
Career Essentials: The Interview
Career Essentials: 3 in 1

Made in United States
North Haven, CT
15 April 2024

51353194R00127